D1079325

MISSION SURVIVAL
CLAWS OF THE
CROCODILE

www.randomhousechildrens.co.uk

CHARACTER PROFILES

Beck Granger

At just thirteen years old, Beck Granger knows more about the art of survival than most military experts learn in a lifetime. When he was young he travelled with his parents to some of the most remote places in the world, from Antarctica to the African Bush, and he picked up many vital survival skills from the tribes he met along the way.

Uncle Al

Professor Sir Alan Granger is one of the world's most respected anthropologists. His stint as a judge on a reality television show made him a household name, but to Beck he will always be plain old Uncle Al – more comfortable in his lab with a microscope than hob-nobbing with the rich and famous. He believes that patience is a virtue and has a 'never-say-die' attitude to life. For the past few years he has been acting as guardian to Beck, who has come to think of him as a second father.

David & Melanie Granger

Beck's mum and dad were Special Operations Directors for the environmental direct action group, Green Force. Together with Beck, they spent time with people who live in some of the world's most extreme places. Several years ago their light plane mysteriously crashed in the jungle. Their bodies were never found and the cause of the accident remains unknown . . .

Brihony Stewart

Beck first met Brihony on a trip to Australia with his parents several years ago, but they have since lost touch. She is a passionate expert on crocodile conservation and likes to think of them as people rather than animals. She may have grown a lot in the years since Beck knew her, but she is still as friendly and likeable as she ever was – if a little blunt at times!

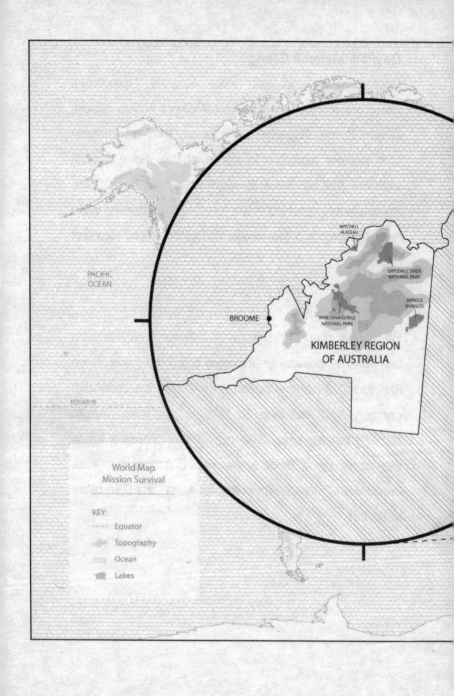

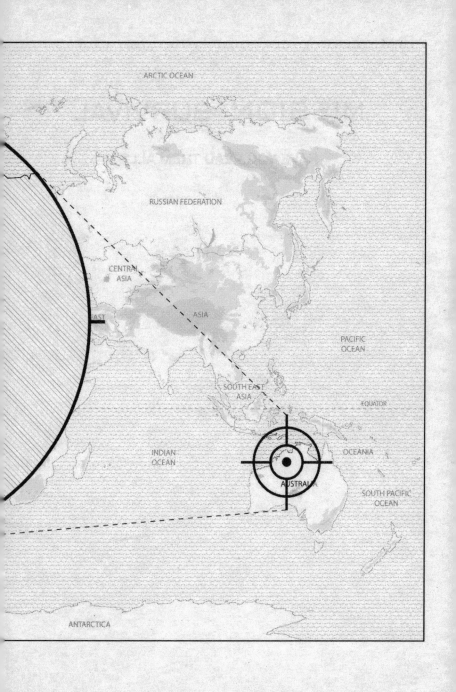

MISSION SURVIVAL

HAVE YOU READ THEM ALL?

GOLD OF THE GODS

Location: The Colombian Jungle

Dangers: Snakes; sharks; howler monkeys

Beck travels to Colombia in search of the legendary City of Gold. Could a mysterious amulet provide the key to uncovering a secret that was thought to be lost for ever?

 WAY OF THE WOLF

Location: The Alaskan Mountains

Dangers: Snow storms; wolves; white-water rapids

After his plane crashes in the Alaskan wilderness, Beck has to stave off hunger and the cold as he treks through the frozen mountains in search of help.

SANDS OF THE SCORPION

Location: The Sahara Desert

Dangers: Diamond smugglers; heatstroke; scorpions

Beck is forced into the Sahara Desert to escape a gang of diamond smugglers. Can he survive the heat and evade the smugglers as he makes his way back to safety?

TRACKS OF THE TIGER

Location: The Indonesian Wilderness

Dangers: Volcanoes; tigers; orang-utans

When a volcanic eruption strands him in the jungles of Indonesia, Beck must test his survival skills against red-hot lava, a gang of illegal loggers, and the tigers that are on his trail . . .

CLAWS OF THE CROCODILE

Location: The Australian Outback

Dangers: Flash floods; saltwater crocodiles; deadly radiation

Beck heads to the Outback in search of the truth about the plane crash that killed his parents. But somebody wants the secret to remain hidden – and they will kill to protect it.

CLAWS OF THE CROCODILE
A RED FOX BOOK 978 1 849 41819 5

First published in Great Britain by Doubleday,
an imprint of Random House Children's Publishers UK
A Random House Group Company

Doubleday edition published 2013
Red Fox edition published 2014

1 3 5 7 9 10 8 6 4 2

Copyright © Bear Grylls, 2013
Cover illustration copyright © Talexi Taini, 2013
Map artwork © Ben Hasler, 2013

The right of Bear Grylls to be identified as the author of this work has been
asserted in accordance with the Copyright, Designs and Patents Act 1988.

All rights reserved. No part of this publication may be reproduced, stored in a
retrieval system, or transmitted in any form or by any means, electronic,
mechanical, photocopying, recording or otherwise, without the prior
permission of the publishers.

The Random House Group Limited supports The Forest Stewardship
Council® (FSC®), the leading international forest-certification organisation.
Our books carrying the FSC label are printed on FSC®-certified paper. FSC is
the only forest-certification scheme supported by the leading environmental
organisations, including Greenpeace. Our paper procurement policy can be
found at www.randomhouse.co.uk/environment

MIX
Paper from
responsible sources
FSC® C016897

Set in Swiss 721 BT

RANDOM HOUSE CHILDREN'S PUBLISHERS UK
61–63 Uxbridge Road, London W5 5SA

www.randomhousechildrens.co.uk
www.randomhouse.co.uk

Addresses for companies within The Random House Group Limited can be
found at: www.randomhouse.co.uk/offices.htm

THE RANDOM HOUSE GROUP Limited Reg. No. 954009

A CIP catalogue record for this book is available from the British Library.

Printed and bound in Great Britain by CPI Group (UK) Ltd, Croydon CR0 4YY

MISSION SURVIVAL

CLAWS OF THE CROCODILE

BEAR GRYLLS

RED FOX

To my sister Lara.

Best friend. Best sister.

I love you.

Chapter 1

Beck Granger is off to Australia!

Beck Granger had typed those words with a song in his heart. Finally, a month into the longest and most boring summer holidays *ever*, something was going to happen.

That was before supper. Now he had come back upstairs and checked his laptop to see how many friends had noticed his new status. He smiled when he saw the first name in the list of comments.

Peter Grey – Awesome sauce! You kept that quiet. Wish I was going with you but parents would have a fit lol.

Peter was his oldest friend from school. Their last two holidays together had been eventful: during the first they had been forced to parachute out of a plane into the middle of the Sahara, escaping from murderous diamond smugglers. On the next one, a volcanic eruption had left them stranded in the Indonesian jungle. Threatened by illegal loggers, tigers and crocodiles, they had finally made their way back to civilization.

Yes, Peter's parents would certainly think twice before letting their son go off with Beck again.

These had been quite normal holidays for Beck. Except for the people trying to kill him. That was a little more unusual.

Beck's earliest memories were of travelling with his parents – before they went missing. The reason was always the same: Beck's father had been Special Operations Director of an environmental organization called Green Force, which worked for change through direct action. Whether it was highlighting the plight of an endangered species, or championing the cause of a native people, or encouraging sustainable development in an area where modern farming was wreaking havoc – Green Force were there at the front line.

The work had taken his parents around the world,

so Beck had found himself with remote tribes in the most extreme spots, from the poles to the equator. And for a white English boy he had proved unusually good at learning how to stay alive. After his parents had vanished, Beck had travelled with his Uncle Al instead.

Now he was in his early teens. When it came to school grades, he knew he would never be more than so-so. When it came to survival, he knew he was up there with the best; but always with more to learn – like how to put up with a long, tedious English summer at home.

He typed a quick reply to Peter. *Didn't know till just now. I'll get you a cuddly koala!*

It had seemed like a good idea to keep the summer break empty. He had enjoyed the rest at first. Spending every night in his own bed. Eating cooked food that you'd actually bought in a shop. No one trying to kill him. These were all things he had felt he needed more of.

But now, halfway through the summer, he was itching for some excitement. He had been spending too much time on PlaceSpace, where his friends shared their holiday plans; he had never imagined that he would be envious of anyone heading for a hotel in Spain.

He had realized how bad it was when he found himself typing out survival advice to Peter:

Look out for hypothermia. It's not just shivering. Your speech gets sluggish and you lose co-ordination . . .

Peter and his family were in a caravan park in Wales. Hypothermia, a fatal cooling of the body's core temperature, was not going to be a problem. *Beck* had the problem. He just wasn't used to being the one stuck at home.

But then Uncle Al had dropped his bombshell.

'How do you fancy a trip Down Under?' he had asked.

Beck had almost cheered. Almost. But one thing he had learned: always get all the facts. And so he had just glanced sideways at his uncle. 'Why . . .?'

Al had smiled at the wary tone. There was always a reason when they went travelling. 'It won't be five-star, I'm afraid. We'll be staying on the Casuarina campus of the University of Charles Darwin. It's all

4

academic stuff. But for you – well, there's beaches, there's the national park, there's sailing . . .'

Al did not have to sell the idea to Beck. Just getting out of the house was enough.

'And what are *you* doing?' Beck asked.

Al looked slightly embarrassed, but pleased at the same time. 'They want to award me an honorary doctorate for my work on the impact of the first Aboriginal people on the prehistoric Australian environment.'

'Cool!' Beck was impressed, and glad for his uncle.

Uncle Al – Professor Sir Alan Granger, to the outside world – had dedicated his life to environmental causes. Becoming Beck's guardian when Beck's parents went missing in an air crash hadn't slowed him down. It wasn't always easy; sometimes it was downright dangerous. Al had upset a lot of powerful people in his time, and Beck reckoned it was only right for his work to be recognized.

'Sure, let's go Down Under!'

It was all too complicated to explain on PlaceSpace. Beck would give Peter the full story the next time they saw each other. He ran his eyes down the list of comments to the next name. What he saw made him sit up.

Brihony Stewart – That's great news! We can catch up. Come and see us in Broome?

Brihony! He hadn't seen her in years – not since . . . well, not since the last trip to Australia. She had been pretty cool, but he still tried not to think much about that particular trip. He had had a great time – mostly. But he had gone out with two parents and come home an orphan.

As representatives of Green Force, Beck's parents had gone out to the Kimberley, the region at the top end of Western Australia, to help an Aboriginal tribe fight a legal case. Beck had been taken under the wing of the tribal elders – once they realized that this English kid really *did* want to learn from them. He had assimilated a huge amount about surviving in the Outback.

What had been the name of his teacher? Pen . . . Pan . . . Pindari, that was it. A tough old guy, really hard to please, so that when you *did* please him, you really felt it had been worth it. His name meant 'high rocks', and he really was as tough as the ancient, sun-baked rocks of the Kimberley. Beck wondered where he was now.

So, yes, a great time . . . up until the moment his parents' plane crashed and Beck's life changed for ever.

Beck called up Google Maps to look up Broome, and also Darwin, where he and Al were going. Darwin was in the Northern Territory, nowhere near the Kimberley.

If Australia was a clock, then Darwin was perched on the north coast at the twelve o'clock position. Broome was at about ten o'clock. It looked no distance at all, but Beck wasn't fooled. The thing he remembered most clearly about Australia was that it was *enormous*. You could drop several United Kingdoms into it and they would just rattle around.

He looked at the scale in the corner of the screen, and saw that there was a good 600 miles between the two places. That was as the crow flies – a very long-distance crow with extra fuel tanks added. Go by road and it was 1,000 miles or more. Australia was big.

So, nice as it would be, he had to accept that he might not be seeing Brihony on this trip. But he didn't want to be negative, and who knew?

So he typed:

Yeah that would be cool. I'll let Al know.

Chapter 2

Twenty-one hours after leaving London, Beck finally managed to get some sleep. After what seemed like five minutes, Al was nudging him out of it. He gestured at the window of the Airbus and spoke in a terrible Australian accent.

'Welcome back, mate! That's the Kimberley out there.'

Beck peered blearily out from a height of 30,000 feet. 'Wow . . .'

Australia just *went on and on*. The vast plains disappeared into the horizon. Dust from the dry, arid ground blended into the haze of the sky so that it was impossible to see the join. The continent seemed to stretch on out over the edge of the world.

He thought again of his last visit. His parents –

and Brihony's – had been helping an Aboriginal tribe called the Jungun to prepare a case to take to the Australian High Court. Two hundred years earlier, an English farmer had taken a liking to some land; he had put a fence around it and claimed it as his own. The Jungun had already been living there for thousands of years, but that was easily taken care of: the farmer had guns and dogs; the Jungun did not.

Two hundred years on, the descendants of those Jungun had sued the descendants of the farmer, claiming their land back.

Beck looked out at the landscape and wondered why anyone was fool enough to think they could own any of it.

He also thought of Brihony. Once again he reminded himself that he wasn't going to the Kimberley this time. He and Al were heading for Darwin. One of the many things Pindari, his Aboriginal mentor, had taught him was not to live in the past. Be in the present; look to the future.

So, here in the present, Beck merely said: 'Was that meant to sound like an Australian?'

'Wasn't it any good?'

'It was great – if all Australians sound like a middle-aged Englishman.'

'If you don't mind, I'm an *elderly* Englishman, and proud of it.'

Beck laughed, and then the captain announced their arrival at Darwin within the hour.

There seemed to be a universal law that said passport queues had to be long and slow and boring. It had been like that in every airport Beck had ever visited, and the one at Darwin International was no exception.

He had turned on his phone a little while ago, and left it to sort itself out with the Australian network. Now, as they slowly shuffled forward, he swiped the screen to unlock it, and casually checked his emails and messages.

The PlaceSpace app notified him of a private message. Brihony again, maybe? He gave the screen a tap.

Jim Rockslide . . .

Beck froze, staring at his phone. It couldn't be! That was impossible! Thoughts whirled around his head. How on earth did a message from Jim Rockslide—

'Beck . . .?' Al said gently, and Beck realized the queue had moved forward a couple of metres without him noticing. He hurried forward, then looked back at the phone. Al asked if something was the matter, but he just shook his head.

The message read: *Jim Rockslide – Friday 31st. Broome. Follow the White Dragon.*

Jim Rockslide? But Jim Rockslide didn't exist!

Jim Rockslide was a made-up character. Beck's dad used to tell him adventure stories about Jim Rockslide, the Hero Geologist who fought Nazis and aliens and smugglers all across the globe.

Beck jabbed at the PROFILE button to find out more about the sender. The profile page was empty, with just the standard outline of a human head instead of a photo. And that made sense, because Beck knew full well that only two people in the whole world had ever heard of Jim. Beck's dad, and Beck himself.

So how was a character made up by a dead man sending messages via PlaceSpace to Beck's phone?

* * *

Beck was still in a daze when they finally passed through passport control. He barely noticed the wait at baggage reclaim or their emergence into the arrivals area. If Al noticed he wasn't saying anything, he probably put it down to jetlag.

Beck's thoughts whirled. He could only think of one way he might have received that message . . .

His father was still alive.

No, he told himself immediately, his father *couldn't* still be alive.

OK, his parents' bodies had never been found, but . . .

But if they *were* still alive, then they must have only *pretended* to be dead all these years. He couldn't think of a single good reason why they would do that. How cruel would that be? What kind of a trick was that to play on their only son?

No, his parents were dead. They *had* to be.

But Jim Rockslide was sending him messages.

Round and round his thoughts went, and eventually one simple certainty came out of it all. Whatever this was about, whoever was sending him those messages . . . Today was Tuesday the 28th.

He needed to be in Broome on Friday the 31st.

'Oh, good grief . . .'

It took Beck a moment to realize that his uncle had said something. Al had got out his tablet as the taxi threaded its way through the suburbs of Darwin on the short trip towards the university. He was checking his own emails. It had been dark by the time they left the airport, so apart from streetlights and the headlamps and red tail-lights of other cars, Beck wasn't seeing much more of Australia.

'What's the problem?' Beck asked.

There was no hiding Al's irritation. 'Some fool – no one you know, but he's a big name – has gone and published a book that contradicts all my research. It's all about the extinction of the megafauna . . . He's wrong, of course, but I'm going to have to completely revise my acceptance speech at the university . . .' He smiled apologetically. 'I'm not going to be great company for the next few days, I'm afraid.'

Beck had no idea what 'extinction of the mega-fauna' meant, and he didn't care. It was like a ray of sunshine into his plans.

He had already checked travel options on his phone. There was a Greyhound coach to Broome every morning. The journey took nearly twenty-four hours.

So he could have tomorrow, Wednesday, to unwind in Darwin. He could travel all day Thursday, and be in Broome by Friday morning. And it wouldn't be like he was travelling into the unknown, because Brihony lived in Broome.

'You know,' he said casually, in a way that immediately made Al alert and suspicious, 'there might be a way around that . . .'

Chapter 3

Coach wheels thrummed along the tarmac. Darwin was far behind. The coach sped like an arrow through the heart of an ancient landscape.

The road was modern, well-maintained and straight. On either side was a shoulder of bare red earth. Then the savannah began – not quite grassland, not quite desert. On the other side of the coach, a sea of knee-high shrubs and bushes stretched into the distance. On Beck's side, it washed up to the foot of red sandstone cliffs the height of a small skyscraper.

Contrary to everything he had predicted, he was back in the Kimberley.

The rainy season, the Wet, would not start for another couple of months. When that happened, the land would be lush, plants would burst out of the soil, and rivers and streams would surge with water. But the last rains had fallen six months ago. The plants were tough and scrubby. The road crossed bone-dry channels that looked thirsty for rain. The land was rugged and hard-baked, able to withstand months and months of dry, hot weather.

The coach was air-conditioned to a pleasant temperature. Outside, the air and land shimmered in the thirty-five-degree heat. The road was the only sign that humans had ever visited this place. It was almost like Australia didn't notice the people who lived in it – though they had been here for over 60,000 years. The Europeans who had named the place Australia were newcomers, turning up over the last couple of centuries. They were the ones who made their mark on the landscape, with their cities and railways and modern highways like this one. Beck had the feeling that if you blinked for a moment, all this could be swallowed up and the land would revert to its natural state. Stark and magnificent and uncaring. It could be a home, but only to people prepared to treat it with respect.

Beck had brought a book to read and music to listen to, but for the time being he sat back to feast his eyes on sandstone bluffs that rose out of the savannah like ancient castles, and landscape that was old when the dinosaurs were still around.

Al had only taken a little persuading. He had looked politely doubtful, but he hadn't said 'no'.

'Sometimes your travels take unexpected turns . . .'

Beck had had all his arguments ready. They were in a First World country, he had pointed out. Yes, the coach would be travelling across some of the most inhospitable terrain on Earth, but the worst that could happen was that it broke down – in which case the driver would radio for help, and that would be that. A few hours and they would be rescued: no need to go walkabout to fetch help. And at the end of the journey was Broome, a modern town. Beck would be met by Brihony's mother – he knew that her father was no longer living with them – who was someone Al knew and trusted.

He felt guilty that he hadn't told his uncle about

Jim Rockslide. Then he told himself that, if he knew, Al would certainly want to come too and would then miss his award ceremony.

Eventually Al had accepted that he was being overcautious. More importantly, he had generously paid for the ticket. And here was Beck on the Greyhound, on his way to find out who this Jim Rockslide was. The only surprise so far had been the colour of the Greyhound: it wasn't grey, but bright red. That was the sort of surprise that Beck felt he could live with.

Beck came awake with a start as the sound of the tyres changed. He was slouched against the window with his cap pulled over his eyes, and he pushed himself upright. The coach was pulling in to a road-side stop: a small shop and some toilets – and beyond that, just miles and miles and miles of Outback.

Beck stepped down, stiff-legged, from the coach. The heat hit him like a sledgehammer as he left the air-conditioned interior. The passengers spread out slowly – some heading for the conveniences; some like Beck just stretching their legs. A few seats back from Beck, a family was travelling with a small toddler. The mother headed into the shop while the father supervised the little boy tottering around the car park. Beck headed for the edge of the tarmacked area, and stood gazing out at the wilderness. It was like the modern world just stopped at his feet. He could take a single step forward and enter a world that hadn't changed for thousands of years.

'Hey, look – roos!'

He dimly heard the comment and glanced back. Sure enough, a small group of kangaroos had emerged from the tall grass at one end of the car park. Kangaroos liked the roads that humans had built. Water collected in the drains, which gave the animals something to drink, and encouraged thick grass for them to eat. Beck didn't know enough about kangaroos to say what kind these were, but he knew their habits. They had scruffy brown fur and were about his height, with sleek, pointed heads and massive thighs.

Some of Beck's fellow passengers aimed their cameras and clicked. The kangaroos lifted their heads from grazing and looked at the humans like they were Martians, then went back to their eating. Beck smiled and looked away.

He checked his watch. The coach would be leaving in five minutes. He ought to use the facilities himself before he got back on board, so he started to stroll towards the building.

Suddenly he stopped in his tracks, stared, and then broke into a run. 'Hey!' he shouted. *'Hey!'*

The father of the little boy was chatting to another passenger and had taken his eyes off him. The child was making a beeline straight for the smallest kangaroo, one hand held out. Beck knew exactly what he was thinking: *Cuddly animal – want to stroke it.*

A larger kangaroo lifted its head suspiciously. Then it hopped towards the boy, raising itself up to its full height. The child kept coming. Beck's feet pounded on the tarmac and he started to shout at the top of his voice, waving his hands in the hope that it might frighten the kangaroo off.

But the animal raised its front legs and balanced on its massive rear feet. Beck grabbed hold of the little boy and whisked him away just as the kangaroo leaped into the air and kicked out with both rear feet. Beck felt the blow whistle past him, but the kangaroo missed. The little boy burst into tears as Beck carried him to a safe distance.

The kangaroo obviously felt it had made its point and went back to its grazing.

The father was now sprinting towards them. 'What the . . . ?'

'They look cute but they're dangerous.' Beck put the boy down, and he promptly ran into his father's arms and started howling. Beck pointed at the smaller kangaroo, then at the one that had attacked the boy. 'That's the joey, the baby, and that's the mother. If you get between them, then the mother will attack. And a blow from those feet could rip a small kid right open.'

The father looked like he had been about to accuse Beck of attacking the child himself, rather than saving his life, but Beck knew he was just in shock.

'Well . . .' he began, and then was distracted by the voice of his wife, who was hurrying across the car park towards them. Beck left it to him to explain how he had taken his eye off their child and almost got him killed.

Welcome to Australia, he thought as he headed for the toilets, *where appearances can be deceiving and even the cute can kill you.*

Chapter 4

There was no coach terminal in Broome. The Greyhound simply drew up outside the Tourist Information Centre on the edge of town. Brihony was waiting, but when Beck staggered off the coach, he managed to look right through her. He had noticed the girl with the shoulder-length auburn hair, but had turned away because he was still expecting to see a little kid.

But then he looked again. The girl had her hands on her hips and was tapping a foot. She craned her neck as she studied each passenger in turn, dismissing those who weren't Beck with an impatient shake of the head.

Then she noticed that he was looking at her, and he saw the realization dawn. She had been doing the same as him – looking for someone much younger.

'Beck . . . ?'

'Brihony . . . ?'

And then they laughed, and it just felt right to give each other a hug.

Brihony's mother was waiting at the back of the crowd. Beck didn't have any difficulty recognizing her, though he could have sworn she was taller when he last saw her. Dr Mia Stewart was like an older, more weathered version of Brihony. The hair was shorter and turning grey. The eyes and the smile were very similar.

'Glad you could come, Beck. Welcome to Broome!'

'Thanks,' he said with feeling. He was mighty glad to have arrived.

Beck had always found that the only thing he disliked about travelling was, well, the travelling. There had been more stops along the way, but fortunately they hadn't met any more angry kangaroos. Every time they stopped he felt a little stiffer and his arms and legs took more persuading to get moving again. And the last twelve hours had been spent in darkness as the coach drove through the night, so there was no landscape to look at – just his own reflection in the windows. He had tried to sleep, but succeeded only briefly.

'The car's this way,' Dr Stewart told him.

The car was a station wagon parked by the kerb. Beck threw his bag into the back. Dr Stewart swung the door closed and he smiled at the sticker in the window. Next to the remains of a tent, a cartoon crocodile with a napkin around its neck was licking its lips. A couple of stick men were fleeing into the distance. Bright letters below the picture announced: DON'T SASS A SALTIE. Under that were the words: SALTWATER CROCODILE CONSERVATION CLUB.

Dr Stewart saw Beck looking at it and laughed. 'Brihony's really getting into crocodile conservation.'

'Yeah, well,' Brihony said casually. 'They've been here for millions of years, and I know all about respecting ancient, scaly people – I mean, animals.'

Her mother pretended to clip her ear, and they got into the car. Beck sat in the back with Brihony as they drove down the long, wide streets. Beck had the feeling that the town had just been plonked there, on a peninsula between the Indian Ocean on one side and Roebuck Bay on the other – a very thin layer of civilization laid down over a continent that barely noticed it. If you dug down a couple of centimetres, you would find native Australia again.

'Did you have a good trip, Beck?' Brihony's mother asked.

'I did, thanks, yes, Dr Stewart,' he said politely. It felt a little awkward to call her that, but he knew she was an expert on Australian wildlife, and if someone has earned the right to be called 'Doctor', it's usually best to stick to it.

'Oh, please, call me Mia!' she laughed. 'I think you're old enough. Ever been to Broome before?'

'No, never.' When he'd visited with his parents, they had stayed with the Jungun – they hadn't got as far as Broome. Beck looked from mother to daughter and wondered whether it was possible that he or his dad had mentioned Jim Rockslide last time. Did the Stewarts know about him? If so, then maybe this was simply a silly joke and no mystery at all. And so he watched carefully for any kind of reaction as he added: 'I had a friend who told me all about it, though. Jim Rockslide.'

Neither of them looked like he had just spoiled their game. Mia was politely interested, but had clearly never heard of him.

Brihony just laughed. 'Good name.'

'Does Jim live here?' her mother asked.

'No. And I've not seen him for years.'

'That's a shame.' No, Beck decided, neither Mia nor Brihony knew anything about Jim. 'Anyway, I'll take you home now – you can get a shower, have some breakfast, and then we'll show you Broome.'

'Thanks,' he said earnestly. 'I'd really like to see it.'

The message had said *Follow the White Dragon*. If he went about asking people about white dragons, then he would probably be locked up. Or he could try to find it for himself, and that meant having a look around.

'You're just in time for the festival,' Brihony added.

'What festival's that?'

'Shinju Matsuri. It's a really big thing around here. It'll be great.'

* * *

A few hours later, Beck was bristling with impatience. He had come to Broome to find Jim Rockslide, not . . . go to the museum . . . walk on the beach . . . or even surf in the Indian Ocean . . . All those things were fun, but none of them helped him with his mission. There was no sign of a white dragon anywhere, and he really didn't want to ask if anyone had seen such a thing.

But he started to feel excited again as they strolled towards Broome's Chinatown for the start of the big parade. Mia had dropped them off, arranging to pick them up an hour later. They heard music all around them. Crowds gathered, laughing and chatting. It was impossible to feel uninspired when so many people were just having a good time.

'*Shinju Matsuri* means "Festival of the Pearl",' Brihony explained. She had to raise her voice to be heard. 'It celebrates all the different cultures that have come together in this town.'

'It sounds Japanese,' Beck said.

'It is. There was a big pearl-fishing industry here, which was started by Japanese divers. But it celebrates all the cultures. Like Chinese – see?'

She pointed, and Beck's eyes went wide. Above the heads of the crowd lining the street he saw a dancing dragon.

It wasn't white. It was red and gold and green, and held up by a dozen people. The head had a pair of flashing eyes, and gaping jaws. The body was long, winding from side to side like a snake. Beck had seen this kind of thing at festivals before.

The dragon danced and swayed to the music, and he felt himself being caught up in the rhythm. After the dragon came floats and a marching band, then more floats and another dragon.

Brihony was telling him more about the festival: how there would be a carnival of the sea on Cable Beach, and a dragon boat regatta out on the bay, and – and something about stairs going up to the moon . . .

But suddenly he was no longer listening. Not to her; not to the music; not to the noise of the revelling crowd. Following the parade he'd seen another dragon. This one was smaller and much less gaudy than the ones that had gone before. It had all the usual tassels and decorations but they weren't coloured. There were no golds, no reds, no yellows, no blacks.

Everything was just white.

Chapter 5

Like all the others, the white dragon swayed and danced to the music. Beck couldn't take his eyes off it. He had travelled over a thousand miles, not knowing what he was looking for, not even sure that it wasn't some kind of stupid joke. But here was a white dragon. He almost expected it to stop in front of him, the dancers to take off their costume and tell him all about it. Whatever 'it' was.

But the message had told him to *follow* the white dragon. That was easy enough, but how was he going to explain it to Brihony?

Brihony solved the problem herself.

'Hey, Beck, fancy a hotdog?'

'Sure! Thanks!' He had to shout to be heard. 'I'll wait here!'

She smiled and said, 'OK,' and ducked into the crowd.

Beck took a deep breath and darted left. He was already following the dragon.

The parade meandered along. Beck was pushing through the people jostling him on all sides, but he was able to keep up with the dragon as it danced to and fro. He strained his eyes for some sort of clue as to what was going on – something about the dragon's decorations, or maybe a glimpse of someone inside it. There was a hidden grille in the dragon's throat that allowed the lead person inside its head to see out, but he couldn't make out the figure. When his eyes met the dragon's, they were just blank and painted.

Then the dragon started to move away from him. To his surprise, Beck realized it was turning into a side street on the other side of the road.

'Hey!' he called. The dragon ignored him, and the parade carried on. The crowd on the other side parted to let the dragon through, and then closed up again. And now Beck was stranded with a wall of people and a moving parade between him and the thing he was after.

He pushed his way through the onlookers on his side of the road, just as a marching band was passing by. Craning his neck and jumping as high as he could to see over their heads, he could just make out the tail end of the white dragon disappearing down the alley. Then the band was past and he hurried after it. He stumbled under the front feet of another dancing dragon, and the operator inside its head had to swerve to avoid him. Beck heard a very human, very irritated 'Out of the way!' in a broad Australian accent, but he had already picked himself up and was pushing through the crowd on the far side.

The alleyway led away from the main street. Then, like so much of Broome, the town just stopped. The alley turned into a dirt track that crossed a stretch of scrub and disappeared amongst some trees. The white dragon was now just a pale shimmer in the gloom – and then it was gone. Beck broke into a run to try and catch up with it. The sounds of the parade – the music, the laughter, the chat – faded away behind him as he sprinted across the open ground. Then he was amongst the trees and saw a single light ahead of him. Thirty seconds later he was in a clearing; in front of him was a warehouse surrounded by an empty car park. The main doors were large enough to accommodate a truck, and a faded sign above them gave the name of a trading company that Beck guessed had probably closed down. But next to the big doors was a normal, person-sized door with a light above it, and it was ajar.

'Hello . . . ?' he called softly. He sidled closer, then pushed the door open and peered round.

Inside the warehouse was a big empty space. The edges were in shadow, but there was a pool of dim orange light in the centre of the floor, where the white dragon costume lay discarded on its side. Next to it stood an Aboriginal man wearing a T-shirt and jeans. He waved abruptly.

'Come on in.'

Beck stepped cautiously into the building, and a voice by his ear said: 'Sorry about all the cloak-and-dagger stuff.'

He spun round and leaped away, but the second man had already pushed the door closed. Beck's heart pounded as he studied him. The stranger was another Aboriginal man. He had thick dark hair, skin the colour of mahogany, and eyes that sparkled with good humour. He wore jeans and a University of Melbourne sweatshirt.

'Our lives would be in danger if anyone saw us talking. That's all our lives. All three of us,' he added.

The man walked past Beck to join his colleague by the dragon costume. A nod of his head and a smile said that Beck should follow him. The smile was friendly despite his ominous choice of words.

'Who are you people?' Beck asked. His heart was still thumping, but less wildly now. He carefully hung back so that he could make a break for the door. Still, he told himself, he was probably in no danger. If they had wanted to harm him, the second man could have hit him on the head and he would never have known anything about it. And why go to all this trouble to lure an English boy into harm's way?

'Told you he wouldn't remember,' said the first man. He was shorter and stockier than his friend and his voice was less warm. If Beck had closed his eyes, he might have thought both men were Australians of European descent.

'Believe it or not, we *have* met before,' said the second man. 'I'm Barega. The last time you were here, I worked with your parents as the go-between with the Jungun. Your dad and I had a beer together most evenings – and once I heard him telling you a story. About Jim Rockslide.'

For a few seconds the years fell away and Beck was a little boy again. He was sitting with his father, listening to the latest exciting Jim Rockslide tale. His father loved the planet, and the Jim Rockslide stories were his way of getting his son interested in it too. The Hero Geologist had been invented when Beck was very small. Every time they were in a new country, his dad thought up new stories based on the countryside around them. He would illustrate them by pointing out different rocks – each millions of years old; each a different shape and colour. They showed what an amazing place planet Earth could be. That was what his father had cared about – a passion he had wanted to pass on to his son.

And yes . . . maybe Beck *did* remember an

Aboriginal man being around too. He remembered because he had been young enough to feel jealous of anyone else who heard these stories, which were special to him and his dad alone.

'Yeah, I think I remember.' He looked at the other guy. 'And what about you?' He felt he was owed an explanation.

'I'm Ganan,' the other man said, 'and my father is the chief of the Jungun. Barega, tell him what this is all about.'

Chapter 6

Barega held out his iPad so that Beck could see the picture on the screen. It was a stretch of river valley. Beck recognized the red sandstone walls of the Australian Outback, but the water was a strange yellow colour and the bushes along the banks were black and withered.

'Believe it or not, this is the Kimberley. This river is so polluted, nothing can live here.'

Barega touched the screen to zoom in on a cluster of dead fish that floated belly-up on the surface. 'Plant and animal life were wiped out for miles. The local Aboriginal people, the Yawuru, were forced to abandon these lands. Their livelihoods had disappeared. They tried to get compensation, but the company blamed it on an act of God: What could they do? they asked. It wasn't their fault there was an earthquake. Wasn't their fault the Yawuru had decided to live there.'

'What company?' Beck asked.

'An outfit called Lumos,' Ganan told him.

'Lumos . . .' said Beck as the memories came flooding back. 'I've come across them before. They tried to destroy my friend Tikaani's village in Alaska so they could build an oil refinery. I didn't expect to run into them on the other side of the world.'

Ganan nodded gravely. 'Big, big corporation – got a finger in every pie. This was the spill-off from a uranium mine in the Kimberley. There was an earthquake and it wrecked the water-containment pools. Thousands of gallons of chemically poisoned water leaked out.'

'But . . .' said Barega. He swiped the screen again, and Beck gasped.

He saw a white man he didn't recognize, but more importantly, the man was standing next to Beck's parents. There they were, smiling at the camera, like they were in the same room, so close he could have touched them. But Barega zoomed in on the stranger before Beck could study the photo properly.

'This guy worked for Lumos and he blew the whistle. He contacted Green Force and said he had evidence that the pools were badly constructed. If the builders had followed the proper design, they would have been earthquake-proof. This man had the paper trail that proved Lumos had used cheap, unqualified builders who didn't know what they were doing. The pools would have been inspected to check that they were up to the right standard, but he also had proof that Lumos had faked the positive reports. So our man handed the evidence over to your dad. Next day, he turned up dead.'

The picture changed for the last time. A burned-out Jeep lay upside down at the bottom of a dry river gorge. Above it was a bridge, the rails shattered where the Jeep had burst through.

'It *could* have been an accident, but your mum and dad weren't taking any chances. They copied the evidence onto a USB stick and gave it to your old friend Pindari for safe-keeping. Then they took the original to show to the media in Sydney. And you know what happened next.'

'The plane crashed,' Beck whispered. Tears pricked behind his eyes. This was all new to him; it was re-opening wounds he thought had healed.

'The plane crashed,' Ganan agreed, 'and Pindari disappeared with the stick into the Outback. End of story.'

Beck stared at him. 'And it just ended there? You couldn't do anything more? You couldn't tell the media, you couldn't tell the police, you couldn't—'

Ganan shrugged. 'Sorry, mate. We needed evidence. We didn't have it. Even if we had the evidence on Lumos's water pools, there was nothing to tie it in to your parents' death.'

'But you think Lumos caused the crash,' Beck whispered. It was one thing to suspect it hadn't been an accident. It had crossed his mind many times. But now, to have someone as good as tell him . . .

'There's no doubt at all,' Barega confirmed. 'Lumos murdered your parents. I'm sorry, Beck. There's no other way to say it. They are dangerous, dangerous people.'

Ganan continued while Beck took this in.

'Meanwhile Lumos launched a massive PR

campaign to paint themselves whiter than white. Green Force could have fought back, but they were in a state of shock following the death of your parents. They decided—'

'Reluctantly,' Barega butted in.

'They decided, *reluctantly*, that they weren't going to win this one. It's one of the few cases Green Force have lost, and they're not proud of it.'

Barega switched off the iPad and put it in his pack.

Beck looked from one man to the other. 'So what's changed? Why are you telling me this now?'

'Lumos are back in the game,' Barega told him. 'They want to build another uranium mine.'

'On our land,' added Ganan. 'On Jungun land. My father, the chief, gets to decide whether to allow it, and he doesn't know what I've just told you.'

'So tell him,' Beck said with a shrug.

Ganan pulled a face as if there was a bitter taste in his mouth. 'He wouldn't believe me. If this goes ahead, then it will make him fantastically rich. And that's all he cares about.'

'We don't want to be fantastically rich,' said Barega. 'This is more important than dollars. We want him to keep the lands for our people. It's our heritage. We've been there for thousands of years, and money in the bank won't bring that back.'

'Basically,' said Ganan, 'we need that evidence. We need that USB stick. To convince the old man and to sway public opinion.'

Beck's head hurt. There was so much to take in. He just wanted to find a corner to curl up in and think for about a million years. He didn't want to pick holes in the men's story – but there were things that still didn't quite add up.

'So . . .' he said slowly, trying to work out what the problem was. 'Find Pindari. Ask him for the stick back.'

The men exchanged exasperated glances.

'Pindari doesn't make appointments,' Ganan said. 'He doesn't have a phone. He doesn't do email. He's barely been seen for years. If he wants to be found, he'll be found.'

'And it's the finding that's the problem.' Barega

looked embarrassed. 'Look, Ganan and I, we both made our choices when we were young. We decided we were going to learn the whitefella's ways, not our own. I went into law. He's an engineer. We went to university and we forgot whatever we knew about our own traditions.'

'He means,' Ganan said bluntly, 'we don't know the old bushcraft ways. We wouldn't know where to begin looking for Pindari. You would.'

'Me?' Beck said in surprise.

'Pindari said you were the best pupil he ever had. He said you had the Dreaming in you. There's no higher compliment he could have paid.'

Beck felt faintly embarrassed by the praise, though he couldn't deny it felt good. But he was still confused.

'But *me*? There must still be some Jungun who know how—'

'We don't want to use anyone from our tribe,' Ganan said abruptly. 'Lumos's money is too tempting. We don't know that one of our people wouldn't track down Pindari, find the USB and just hand it over to the corporation.'

'And there's no guarantee Pindari would let them have it anyway,' said Barega. 'It takes a lot to earn his trust, but you . . .'

And just as he said 'you', there was a noise at the door. Beck's senses and emotions were already tuned to max and it was like a rifle shot echoing inside the warehouse.

Chapter 7

He whirled round to face the door. Both men moved more quickly than Beck would have thought possible. Ganan darted off into the gloom at the edges of the warehouse; Barega leaped over to the wall and swiped at a light switch. The warehouse was plunged into darkness. While Beck was still rooted to the spot in confusion, a rectangle of light appeared as someone pulled the door open. Two silhouettes struggled together, and angry shouts echoed around the walls.

'*Let me go! Let me . . .*'

Beck recognized the voice. 'Hey, that's Brihony! It's all right!'

The figures stopped struggling. There was a click, and the lights came on again. Barega kept his hand on the switch. Over by the door, Ganan and Brihony were still locked in each other's arms. They stared suspiciously at each other, then slowly backed apart.

'Miss Stewart,' Barega called. 'Come on in.'

'How much did you hear?' Ganan asked brusquely.

She turned to face him, hands on hips. 'Lumos, parents murdered, USB stick, Beck the best tracker you've got . . . Did I miss anything?'

'No.' Barega's friendly grin was a sharp contrast to Ganan's scowl. 'I think you got it all.'

'And is Lumos really that dangerous?' The question was aimed at the two men, but she glared at Beck as she said it.

His mind was still dazed with everything he had learned and he couldn't meet her eye. He just looked at the floor while the others talked around him.

'It really is,' Barega assured her.

'We have contacts inside the corporation,' said Ganan, after a pause. He was evidently struggling with how much to tell her. 'Lumos have been keeping tabs on Beck ever since his parents died. Now that he's in Broome, they'll think he's come in search of the hidden evidence. They'll never allow that – and remember, they've already killed at least once.'

Beck opened his mouth to speak; Brihony interrupted him.

'If Beck's in danger in Broome, it's only because you guys brought him here.'

'Um . . .' Beck began, and she turned on him.

'Oh, please, don't say you came here to see me!' Back to the men: 'If you really cared, you'd have left him alone and found someone else to do your tracking.'

Beck was growing tired of being talked about as if he wasn't there. 'Brihony, thanks,' he said, 'but this really isn't your problem. I'm in it because of my parents. But you . . . No, you're not involved, and I'm sorry I got you into it this far. The best you can do is—'

'The best I can do, Beck Granger, is stand by my friend – if you're going along with this. Are you?'

Three pairs of eyes settled on Beck and he felt his face burn. He knew what he wanted to do. He wanted to rush out into the Outback and bring his parents' killers to justice. On the other hand . . .

'It's kind of a lot to take in. And I promised my uncle I wouldn't get caught up in any more adventures.'

Ganan looked as if he was about to remonstrate, but Barega just patted him on the shoulder.

'It *is* a lot to take in. You two, get yourselves back home. Beck, think about it. Jim Rockslide will get in touch to ask what you decide.'

'But,' Ganan added harshly, 'you cannot tell anyone about this. Got that? *Anyone*. Lumos have stooges in the police, in the government . . . they are everywhere.'

It was quite dark when they left the warehouse and walked back towards the town.

'Well, I got you that hotdog,' Brihony said tightly.

Beck felt his face begin to burn with guilt again. He knew he had treated her badly. He hadn't told her the truth about why he had come to Broome, and then he had deserted her. But he knew that even though she was hurt, she had heard enough to understand that he had been presented with some hard choices.

Beck had almost forgotten there was a festival going on. The parade was over now, and the crowd was dispersing. No one paid any attention to the teenage boy and girl walking along in silence.

'There you are!' Mia was pushing her way towards them through the crowd. She didn't seem to notice their silence. 'Come on, or we'll miss it.'

'Miss what?' Brihony asked.

Mia gave her a look of fond exasperation. 'The staircase to the moon! Come on!'

Beck followed along behind. Staircase to the moon? What was that about? Brihony had said something about it earlier, but right now he really didn't care. He had so many more important things to think about.

Mia drove them to Town Beach. This was on the southern, Roebuck Bay side of town, and they weren't alone. It wasn't as crowded as the festival, but there were still plenty of people about. The delicious smells from the food stalls reminded Beck that he hadn't had a proper meal yet. The tide was out, revealing a series of mudflats that sloped down to the water. The moon was low on the horizon to the east, but it was hidden by clouds so all that could be seen was a glow.

'I hope it comes out,' Mia worried. 'It would be a shame to miss it . . .' Then she spotted a friend, and hurried over to have a chat.

For a moment Beck and Brihony were alone together. Beck knew it might be his only chance to say what he had to say. He looked Brihony in the eye. 'I'm sorry I wasn't straight with you.'

She just stared back and let him talk.

'Look, I've decided. I'm going to tell Al about all this, and he can talk to the guys. He's involved too – I mean, my dad was his brother. And he knows people. He could get a proper professional tracker in to find Pindari – and then, if they still need me to ask him to hand the stick over, they can come and get me. I made Al a promise and I'm going to keep it.'

Slowly, Brihony smiled, and Beck knew he was forgiven. He also felt as if a great weight had been lifted from his shoulders. He couldn't be expected to solve all the world's problems.

She turned towards the silver glow in the sky. 'Look,' she said. 'It's coming out.'

The clouds had drifted away and a full moon shone down on Broome. The crowd gasped and cheered, and then Beck saw it.

The mudflats weren't completely smooth. They ran in ripples, parallel to the shore. They were wet, and the moon picked out a golden path across them towards the onlookers. But only the tips of each ripple caught the light; the dips were in shadow. And so a series of golden stripes ran out from the shore towards the moon across the bay. It really did look like a staircase.

'Wow,' Brihony breathed. 'Isn't that amazing?'

Despite everything whirling around in his head, Beck felt a grin tugging at the corners of his mouth. 'Yes, it is.'

It was spectacular. It was one more example of the amazing things that the Earth could do. There were still evil men out there, and his parents had still been murdered, but right then he was just glad to be alive and well on this amazing planet, in the company of a good friend.

Mia was standing behind them now. 'I'm so glad you got to see that, Beck! Come on, let's get something to eat . . .'

They bought some boxes of freshly cooked, spicy noodles and carried them away to a quiet spot in the dunes: a hollow surrounded by scrub grass, cut off from all the sights and sounds of Broome.

'OK,' said Mia, 'sit down, make yourselves comfortable . . . Oh, hello.'

Two men were coming down the other side of the hollow. They were just dark silhouettes against the light sand – Beck couldn't make out their features.

Then one of the men flashed a torch straight into Mia's face and spoke in a harsh voice: 'One chance, lady. Where's the USB stick?'

Mia blinked angrily against the light. 'Do you mind . . . ? What are you talking about—?'

Something whistled through the air. There was a dull thud, like the sound of someone kicking a block of wood. Mia cried out and dropped to the ground. In the torchlight, Beck saw red blood streaming down the side of her head.

The man stood over Mia. He was powerfully built, with wide shoulders and muscles that strained against his clothing. He and his colleague both wore balaclavas and twirled baseball bats.

Beck was dazzled as the torch was turned on him and Brihony. They clung together as the two men moved closer.

'Same question,' the first man said. 'Where's the USB stick?'

Chapter 8

The men advanced. Beck and Brihony, hearts pounding, slowly retreated. Mia lay on the sand, unmoving. Beck strained to see through the darkness. Did her head just twitch? He wasn't sure. She was probably only unconscious, not dead, but he knew something about blows to the head. It wasn't like on TV, where you woke up after a few minutes and felt as right as rain. Anything with the power to knock you out was serious, and if she had been hit with a baseball bat, then she could have a fractured skull, internal bleeding . . .

The man slapped his bat into a gloved hand with a slow, menacing beat. 'Right, kids – we can do this my way or we can do it the hard way. Just give us the USB stick and we'll be gone.'

Beck swallowed to clear his dry throat. There was no doubt who these men worked for, but they had got their facts wrong. Pindari had the USB stick; he didn't. But if he told them that, the men would just think he was trying to bluff again.

'Look,' he started to say, 'we don't—'

'OK.' The man sounded resigned. 'Hard way it is. My friend here will start at Dr Stewart's feet and work his way up until you tell us something interesting.'

The second man strolled over to where Mia lay, raised his bat over her feet and started to bring it down.

'*OK!*' Brihony screamed. The bat stopped a centimetre from Mia's ankles. 'OK. OK.' She bravely took a couple of deep breaths. Her voice trembled, but she made a good effort to control it. 'It's in my mum's handbag.' She pointed. 'Over there.'

Beck carefully kept a straight face, not giving anything away. Mia had put the handbag down on the sand just before the men showed up. He didn't know what Brihony was playing at, but if she had any kind of plan, then it was more than he had. And maybe there *was* a USB stick in Mia's handbag. It wouldn't be the one they were after, but how would they know that just by looking at it?

At a nod from his colleague, the second man picked up the handbag and passed it to Brihony.

'Empty it onto the ground.'

Brihony did as she was told, though her fingers shook as she tugged at the zip. She upended the bag, and the contents spilled out onto the sand. The man shone his torch down on the small pile and Beck looked closely. Purse, lipstick, small packet of hankies, phone . . . Nothing that looked like a USB stick.

The second man crouched down and poked through the pile while the first kept his guard over the two friends. He looked up.

'It's not here.'

'Oh, for crying out loud, you stupid drongo!' Brihony snapped. She strode forward, ignoring the threatening gesture from the first man, and rummaged quickly through the pile herself. 'Here it is – right here. Look.'

She had something small and cylindrical in her hand. She held it out towards the second man, covering it with her fingers. As he leaned forward, she pressed the top, and a jet of fluid squirted into his eyes.

He howled and staggered backwards, clutching at his face. The first man leaped forward, but he tripped over Mia and stumbled, straight into another squirt of the fluid. He bellowed and fell backwards into his companion, and they collapsed into a tangled heap on the sand.

'Come on.' Brihony grabbed Beck's hand and pulled him away. He hadn't realized she was sobbing. 'Come on . . .'

He threw a last glance back at Mia. It felt heartless to leave her just lying there, needing medical attention. But there was nothing he could do while these two guys were around.

They scrambled up the sides of the hollow and ran over the dunes, away from the sea.

'What was that stuff?' he gasped.

'Anti-assault spray.'

'Neat.'

The soft sand meant that every step was a stumble. After a minute, Beck glanced back again.

The men were only just emerging from the hollow. The moon had stayed out, and Beck knew that their dark figures would be very visible against the light sand.

They had to get to help. They were in a town of 15,000 people – it shouldn't be hard! The problem was that their attackers were between them and the crowd. He and Brihony were running away from any potential helpers. They couldn't just change direction and find some witnesses. The men would just cut across and intercept them before anyone else was within earshot.

The ground grew harder beneath their feet, and buildings loomed up ahead of them. They could run more easily now. Unfortunately, this meant that the men would be able to as well. With their longer strides they would soon catch up. Beck and Brihony had to take advantage now, while their pursuers were still struggling through the sand.

Ahead of them were shops and stalls, but they were closed.

'What is this place?' Beck asked.

'Apex Park. This is where Mum parked. We've got to get back to the car.'

'Can you drive?'

'No, but my phone's in it . . .'

Beck glanced back and saw that the men were gaining on them now.

Suddenly he and Bryony were running on tarmac: the car park. It was almost empty, and Mia had parked at the far end. Beck didn't bother looking back because it would only slow him down. The car was still miles away, and another problem occurred to him: hadn't Mia locked it? How were they going to get in?

And then they were there. Beck tugged at the nearest door. Sure enough, it was locked. He turned round: the men were almost upon them.

Brihony was fumbling inside the front wheel arch. Suddenly the car's lights flashed as the remote locking system operated.

'Spare key in a magnetic box!' she said, waving it triumphantly under Beck's nose. Beck dived into the back of the car and pulled the door shut behind him.

Brihony only had her door half closed when the first man caught up. He grabbed it and began to pull it open again. There was a brief tug-of-war, and then

Brihony deliberately let go. All at once the door swung open and he fell over backwards. She grabbed the handle again and pulled it shut, just as the second man reached them. He made the mistake of taking hold of the edge just as the door was slamming shut, and it closed on his fingers. He bellowed with pain, and staggered away. Brihony pressed the central locking switch, and all four doors locked with a loud click.

Beck watched the men nervously. He knew that car glass was tough, but he didn't feel secure when it was all that stood between him and a baseball bat. He scrambled into the front passenger seat while Brihony fumbled with her phone.

'Police? Hi, yeah, I'm in Apex Park and two guys are—'

One of the men brought his bat down on the window. The glass splintered and starred, but stayed intact.

'Did you hear that? Yeah, I'm locked in a car and there's two men attacking us. Also they knocked my mother out – she's lying on the beach and she'll need an ambulance—'

The man swung the bat at the window again, and it gave a little more. Beck slammed his hand down on the car horn, over and over. The sound echoed around the car park. Surely someone would come and investigate?

'Yeah, that's my friend . . .' Brihony said into the phone.

The men were still out there, though they backed off when the horn started. They shot anxious glances into the dark, torn between wanting to get at the two kids in the car, and wanting to escape before help came. They circled the car like wolves waiting at the base of a tree for their prey to fall out.

But Beck kept blasting the horn, and finally they heard the sound of the siren. The man with the bat smashed it against the car once more, but it was just frustration. He and his colleague turned and ran off into the darkness only seconds before the police car pulled up.

Beck and Brihony didn't unlock the doors until they saw a uniformed police officer emerge.

Chapter 9

'And you didn't get a look at their faces? Either of them?' the policewoman asked.

Brihony silently shook her head.

Mia lay unconscious on the other side of a glass partition. A doctor and a nurse fussed over her, and she was being fed oxygen. The doctors had assured them that this was normal procedure. Giving a patient extra oxygen just meant that the body was getting as much oxygen saturation as possible to aid its recovery.

'Can you think of any enemies your ma might have? Has she had an argument with anyone recently? Anyone at work?'

Brihony shook her head again. 'No one.'

In the few moments between the men running off

and the police arriving, Beck and Brihony had come to an agreement. The police would ask questions, but they wouldn't mention Lumos. Ganan had said that the corporation even had people in the police. Talking about them might mean putting people in real danger.

The doctor stepped out of the room behind them. He had a warm, reassuring smile which Beck felt was probably genuine.

'Brihony? Here's the deal. Your mum has a hairline fracture to the skull, and there's almost certainly bruising to the brainstem. But her vital signs are good. She will probably be unconscious for two or three days, but that's normal. It just means she's getting better. Then, when she wakes up, she'll need to stay in for monitoring. The important thing is, she's through the worst. Every day from now on will be an improvement.'

Brihony was silent for a moment. She stood with her eyes closed and relief on her face, taking in the good news. 'I suppose there's no reason to stay around, then?' she asked.

'That's up to you. You're welcome to wait here,

but it can get mighty boring. Do you have some-where you can go? What about your dad? We should get in touch with him.'

'He doesn't live with us, and he's away at the moment,' Brihony told him.

'Two kids can't just go home alone,' the police-woman said. 'Is there someone we can contact to come and get you? Another family member? A friend?'

Brihony opened her mouth, but Beck got in first.

'It's OK, thanks. I'll call some friends.'

Brihony closed her mouth and nodded to back him up. The policewoman looked a little surprised, maybe wondering why the boy with the English accent was calling the shots.

'Well, if you're sure. If you remember anything else, get in touch; otherwise we'll just have to wait for Dr Stewart to wake up so we can talk to her.'

And good luck if you do, Beck thought. Mia knew nothing about Lumos – she would have no idea who could have done this. The thought made him boil with rage. The men had mentioned the USB stick, so there was no question who they worked for. But

Lumos were stupid if they thought that he and Brihony already had it. They weren't just murdering thugs, they were *stupid* murdering thugs. And that made them even more dangerous, because who knew where they would lash out next?

Brihony waited until the policewoman was out of earshot, then turned to Beck. 'You're going to do it, aren't you?' she asked quietly. 'You're going to find Pindari . . .'

He nodded. 'This is something I have to do. And not just for those who want to protect this land – I have to do it for me too. And for Mum and Dad.'

Beck had thought hard about this. On the one hand, he had promised Al to stay out of trouble. On the other, Mia had been badly hurt, and maybe other people would be too if Lumos weren't stopped. Whoever had killed his parents were still out there and might strike again. Meanwhile, if Ganan was to be believed, Lumos had people everywhere. No one and nowhere was safe. Beck couldn't bring his Uncle Al into this mess – too many people that Beck loved had already been hurt.

If it was up to him to stop it, then that was what he would do. Alone.

'Can I borrow your phone?' he asked Brihony. 'Mine's at your house.'

He used it to log on to PlaceSpace and send a message to Jim Rockslide.

Barega and Ganan picked them up from the hospital and drove at random through the town. They didn't go back to Brihony's house – Ganan pointed out it was quite possible that Lumos were watching it.

'First thing,' said Beck, 'you want me to find Pindari? I need to know roughly where to start. Australia's kind of big.'

'You'd noticed that too?' Barega smiled, though Ganan scowled at him for making a joke at a time like this. 'No worries. We can take you to his usual territory.'

'Cool. Second . . .' Beck gestured at what he was wearing – a T-shirt, baggy shorts and trainers. 'This is completely unsuitable for the desert and I didn't bring any proper gear. You'll have to get me some clothes – and make sure you've got the same things.

Long-sleeved shirts, trousers, and everything needs to be loose-fitting – to let air circulate but prevent sweat from evaporating too quickly. Wide-brimmed hats. Sturdy boots.'

'How about supplies?' Ganan asked.

'High-energy food concentrates, and plenty of water. In a climate like this we'll lose three and a half litres per hour.'

'We'll be near a river,' Barega pointed out. 'Water's no problem.'

'As long as we can purify it. We'll need bottles – and I mean proper, large, five-litre ones, not those tiny little things you get in shops. If we're striking out inland, we'll need to take a proper supply with us.'

'No worries,' Ganan said. 'But nothing happens until after sun-up and we've all had some sleep.' By now it was past midnight and sleep was a welcome idea. 'We've got a room rented. It'll be crowded but it'll be safe, and Lumos shouldn't know about it.'

'But first thing in the morning,' Brihony said, 'you can take me back to my place – just long enough to pick up my clothes.'

Beck stared at her. 'Eh?'

She gazed calmly back at him, but for a moment her voice trembled. 'Beck Granger, do you think, after what's happened, that I'm just going to sit back and twiddle my thumbs? In case you hadn't noticed, my mum nearly had her brains smashed in, and I want to get the guys who did it!'

Beck had to admit she had a point. He wanted to get at the people who had killed his parents – it was the same thing. But even so . . .

'Hey, Brihony, no offence, but we can't afford passengers,' Ganan said.

Her eyes flashed with anger. 'Can't afford passengers? You two are already passengers! You said it yourself – Beck is the one with the expertise! He's the one in charge!'

'Right!' Beck agreed. 'And that's why I say there's no way I'm going to put you in danger . . .'

Chapter 10

'You know,' said Barega with a broad smile, 'you two are going to have to start talking to each other again eventually.'

Beck and Brihony scowled at each other, and looked away again. The boat continued its steady chug up the river gorge.

Beck knew, deep down, that Brihony was right. She had run through all her points while all three of them tried to persuade her that she shouldn't be coming. Lumos's thugs could very easily strike again. She couldn't stay at the hospital for ever. If she went to stay with her dad when he returned, then he would be in danger too. At home on her own, she would be twice as vulnerable. The police had no reason to believe that she was at risk, so she wouldn't get any protection. Coming with Beck and Ganan and Barega was the only logical course.

But Beck didn't like losing arguments. And deep down he was scared that someone else close to him would wind up getting hurt.

'We're going to be roughing it,' he reminded Brihony. 'It'll be hot, we'll be tired and thirsty . . .'

'I know all about roughing it in the Outback, thanks. I've been camping more times than I can remember.'

Beck sighed and dropped the subject. He recognized a losing battle when he saw one.

They had stuck together as a foursome, not splitting up. Brihony and Beck had got a few snatched hours of sleep on the floor of the men's shared room. Then it was breakfast in a diner, before Beck supervised the buying of clothes and supplies. It was scary to think that he was in charge of keeping the four of them alive.

But at least he looked the part – in a long-sleeved cotton shirt and a pair of sturdy cargo trousers, with extra outside pockets and vents down the legs to help the air circulate. On his head was a wide-brimmed hat made of sheep leather, which blocked out the sun and kept his face and shoulders in permanent shade.

He had insisted that everyone had their own water bottle. His own dangled at his side, tied to a long strap that went across his body. On his belt hung a machete – a thirty-centimetre blade of hard, shiny steel with a pointed tip, one edge blunt, the other razor-sharp. Pindari would no doubt have scorned it, he thought; the old man would have said his people had survived for thousands of years without such things. But Beck was not an Aboriginal boy, and a machete had kept him alive on more than one occasion. He wasn't going into the Outback without one.

Like Beck, the two men wore brand-new clothes. Brihony had found all the right kit in her cupboard at home. It had been a tense five minutes of waiting outside while she got it – running in, throwing things into a bag and running out again. Still, Beck was glad they had done it. It had also meant that he could retrieve his phone – along with something else that now hung around his neck on a bootlace.

Beck's fire steel was his oldest possession, given to him by his father years ago. He could even say it was his oldest friend. It consisted of a short rod and a flat piece of steel. The rod was made of a substance called ferrosium, a combination of metals that sprayed sparks when it was struck with another piece of metal. The flat bit of steel was what you did the striking with. Even if it was soaking wet, the ferrosium could spray sparks like a hose sprays water. Beck had used it to light camp fires for himself all over the world – from jungles to the Arctic. When it hung around his neck again, the metal cold against his skin, he had finally felt properly dressed for the expedition.

Ganan and Barega had acquired a small boat from somewhere, and then they had all headed inland in a four-by-four, towing it on a trailer. First they had followed a proper highway, then turned off onto rutted dirt tracks. Finally they had reached the river, which was the best way to get to Pindari's land.

The boat had an outboard motor and a canopy to

shade them. The men sat in the stern while Brihony and Beck took the middle seat. The supplies they had brought with them were piled up in the bows – boxes of canned food, bottles of water, sleeping bags and tents.

The river was a dirty, muddy brown, but even after six months of nothing but sun and baking heat it was still deep. It snaked through a landscape of red sandstone cliffs and gorges. Under the cliffs there was flat shoreline on either side, though Beck knew that during the Wet, the entire channel would be covered by surging water.

The sky was a blue dome from horizon to horizon. Heat beat down on the canopy, and even the breeze felt like a hairdryer blowing on Beck's face. Once again, he marvelled at how quickly you could shake off civilization in this country. They had parked by the river, slid the boat into the water, set off – and five minutes later, it was as if they had travelled back in time by millions of years. There was nothing to suggest that other humans existed anywhere in the world.

Brihony stiffened suddenly, peering ahead. 'Steer

to the right a bit, Ganan,' she called urgently.

'Why?' he asked, and Beck saw Brihony's look of irritation. Ganan still saw Brihony as an unnecessary passenger.

'Because there's a crocodile dead ahead.'

Chapter 11

The boat swerved abruptly to the right as Ganan pushed the tiller over, and Beck had to grab onto his seat to stay upright. He craned his neck to peer ahead but couldn't see anything apart from the usual stretch of dark brown water.

'Which type of crocodile?' Ganan asked.

'Saltie,' Brihony told him. 'What else?'

Barega came forward to where they sat, one hand on the side of the boat to steady himself. Like Beck, he was studying the water in front of them. 'I don't see it.'

'That's the point,' she replied with tight-lipped patience. 'You don't see the salties. *They* see *you*.'

Although 'saltie' was short for saltwater crocodile, Beck knew that these creatures could just as easily live in fresh water like this river. And then he saw it.

It wasn't much – just the slightest disturbance in the water ahead. It could have been the tip of a log floating just beneath the surface – two black blobs about thirty centimetres apart. They were the crocodile's eyes. The rest of it was invisible. Even though it could only have been a few centimetres beneath the surface, there was no sign of the long, powerful reptilian body.

Brihony had to point it out to Barega, who showed it to Ganan, who carefully steered the boat around it.

'Doesn't look too aggressive,' Barega commented.

Brihony smiled. 'They never do, until they launch an attack. And by then it's usually too late . . .'

'How big do they get?' Ganan asked.

'About five metres long.' Brihony's voice grew warmer as she talked about a subject close to her heart. 'But they can reach six or even seven and weigh four hundred and fifty kilos.'

Beck whistled. Five metres of pure killing machine lurked beneath the water. He had seen them before in the wild and never ceased to be amazed. But wherever they were in the world, and however big, crocodiles tended to have similar habits. They had been around since the age of the dinosaurs, and had used all that time to perfect their predatory nature. They were immensely strong, and they could go a long time without eating. They were cunning and patient. Looking at a croc in a concrete pen in a zoo, you might not see that they were masters of camouflage. It was easier to believe when you were trying to spot one in dark brown croc-coloured water.

The eyes of the saltie disappeared behind them, though Beck was sure it was watching them until they were out of sight.

'Should have brought a gun,' Ganan muttered.

Brihony swung round. 'How can you say that? What have they ever done to you?'

'Nothing,' he replied with a leer, 'and I intend to keep it that way.'

'Crocs eat what they need. They take weak and sick animals—'

'You mean, the ones who don't get out of the way in time?'

'Exactly! They're part of the environment. Other

animals can co-exist with them just fine. All except stupid humans. There's huge pressure on the population. Poachers are after them because saltie hides are worth more than any other type, and no one cares because as far as everyone else is concerned, they're just mindless killers.'

Ganan was grinning, and Beck realized with irritation that he had deliberately wound Brihony up just to get a reaction.

But it was Barega who rebuked him. 'All right, Ganan, cut it out!'

Suddenly Beck turned and saw that the boat was heading straight for the shore. 'Look out!'

Ganan had been enjoying watching Brihony lose her cool so much that he had forgotten he was steering. He pulled on the tiller, and the boat swung round again to head back towards the middle of the channel.

As he did so, Barega almost fell over the side. 'Hey, watch it!'

'Sorry,' Ganan muttered.

The boat resumed its course. Beck settled down next to Brihony again and rolled his eyes. 'And it's not like they attack boats anyway!'

Brihony paused before answering. 'Not often.'

'Huh?'

'They don't attack boats often.'

Ganan stared. 'So they *do* attack boats?'

'It's not the boats they're after – it's the meat steering them. And if they're hungry and you give them an opportunity, they will take you. And it's not a nice way to go. Trust me.'

Everyone took turns as the boat went on, either resting or steering or sitting in the bows to keep a lookout. In the dark water it would be easy to miss an obstacle beneath the surface until it was too late. It would do the boat no good at all to hit a hidden log; and if the log turned out to be a crocodile . . .

For food they munched on dried fruit bars washed down with precious water. They would have a proper meal at the end of the day, but for now too much food would only dehydrate them. Beck made sure everyone kept drinking regularly, even when Barega and Ganan said they weren't thirsty.

'You need one and a half litres per day even when you're just sitting still,' he said. 'When you're moving on foot in this heat, you need that per hour. So just be grateful the boat's doing all the hard work – for the time being.'

Ganan had a map but preferred to navigate by GPS. Beck kept one eye on the map too, matching the marked bends and curves to the reality of the landscape around them. The map showed that they were on the edges of Jungun territory – but it would be another few hours before they were near where Pindari was likely to be.

There were still no signs of any other humans, but as the hours passed they saw wildlife a-plenty. Pointing it all out to Beck, Brihony had soon completely forgotten their disagreement.

Some sleek green birds flew overhead in formation like a squadron of space fighters. Their bodies were shaped like arrowheads with a long, spearlike beak at the end.

'Bee-eaters,' Brihony told him.

Beck watched and marvelled at the way they circled together, never colliding, always knowing exactly where other members of the flock were as they swooped and fed on insects too small for him to see.

Three or four kangaroos were sheltering at the base of a cliff. They took exception to the echoes of the boat's engine and hopped away to a safe distance. They seemed to expend no energy at all, but each leap covered a couple of metres.

At one point they passed a pair of dingoes – wild dogs with ginger fur that was short and stiff, and always made Beck think of a crew-cut. Their heads were lowered as they lapped the water but they watched the boat, ears pricked suspiciously, until it had gone by. Further up the same beach, a monitor lizard plodded along the stones. It walked like a robot, one stiff leg in front of the other, oblivious to anyone or anything that didn't disturb it. Beck didn't doubt the dingoes could have given it a hard time if they felt hungry – but then, it would have given them a hard time back. Wildlife in the Outback, like everywhere else, lived in equilibrium. Everything busy just surviving.

But seeing the dingoes made Beck think. They usually avoided the heat of the day, only coming out at dawn and dusk. He glanced up. The sun was already below the edges of the river gorge. He checked his watch, and cursed himself. He was out of practice. He was meant to be the expedition's Outback expert and he had forgotten the simple fact that when you were this close to the equator, the sun went down very quickly. They had little more than half an hour of daylight left.

'We should call it a day,' he said.

Ganan grunted. Everyone had taken their turn at the tiller as the day went on, but for now he was back in charge. 'We've a couple more hours of daylight. We should keep going.'

'Sure there's daylight,' Beck pointed out, 'but we need what's left of it to set up camp. And down here it's going to get dark sooner.'

Ganan shrugged. 'We've got GPS. The screen lights up.'

Beck kept a hold on his temper. 'GPS doesn't show hidden sandbanks, or rocks, or logs, or crocodiles. It's dangerous to go on. Just trust me, please.'

Barega had been in the front of the boat. Now he came back to join them. 'Hey, what's happening?'

Beck and Ganan spoke simultaneously:

'He won't pull over—'

'Beck doesn't want to go on—'

'Oh, for crying out loud!' Brihony exclaimed. 'How about a compromise? Say, we go on for half an hour?'

Beck shook his head. 'Even half an hour will make it too dark . . .' And then he realized that all four of them were clustered together at the back of the boat. He looked from one to the other.

'Hey, who's keeping a lookout?'

There was a crunch and a smash, and the boat lurched. Barega staggered and fell against Ganan. Ganan fell against the tiller and the throttle, so that the engine suddenly roared and the boat turned at full speed. It was like having the ground pulled from under your feet. Beck and Brihony didn't have a chance. With their arms waving frantically, trying to catch hold of thin air, they toppled backwards over the side and into the water.

Chapter 12

The river closed over Beck's head. Bubbles and engine noise roared in his ears. He lunged furiously for the surface and emerged into the air. Water streamed down his face and plastered his hair over his eyes.

Brihony was just breaking the surface in a fury of splashes. A couple of metres away, the log that they had smashed into swirled gently in the current. The boat still lurched about, heading towards the other bank. The men were desperately trying to reach the throttle.

Beck had one thing on his mind: crocodiles. He looked around. The nearest bank was about twenty metres away.

'Swim for the shore,' gasped Brihony.

'No, no,' Beck shouted. 'Go underwater!'

'Eh?' She looked at him, aghast. 'There could be crocs!'

'Exactly! Trust me!' And to make his point, he jack-knifed and dived down beneath the water.

For a second, Brihony stared at the ripples where Beck had been. Then she followed suit and struck out for the bank with a powerful breaststroke.

It was impossible to see anything. The engine made a dull throbbing beneath the surface, and the water was full of other noises – clicks and bubbles and whirrs. Beck tried not to imagine five metres of reptilian armour-plated teeth and claws heading towards him. He would never see it if it happened.

The water bottle around his neck was part empty and acted like a float, trying to pull him back up. The temptation to get rid of it was strong, but Beck knew that if he did so, he might just be condemning himself to a slower death.

He had to swim up to the surface to take a breath, and saw that he was only about a quarter of the way to the bank. He filled his lungs and ducked under again.

Beck thrust hard with his legs like a frog to push himself through the water. His boots were heavy and just slowed his feet down.

If a crocodile came for him, he wondered what it would feel like. Those jaws could snap his spine and crush his lungs in a second. Then the croc would drag him off to an underwater lair and pin his body under a rock or a fallen tree to rot. That was how they ate. Their jaws were powerful, but they couldn't chew. They had to wait until the food was falling apart. Then they brought it to the surface and tilted their heads back so that the food literally fell into their stomachs. A bad way to go . . . He shook the image from his mind.

Beck suddenly felt the mud at the bottom of the river. Immediately he brought his legs down so that he could run out of the water. Brihony was right behind him, and they lurched towards the shore in a cloud of splashing spray. Once they were out of the water, they kept running until they were at the base of the sandstone cliff. Then they stopped to look back.

Across the river, Barega and Ganan finally had the

boat under control, but it sat much lower in the water now. It listed so that the bow was almost submerged. They were reversing towards the opposite shore.

Beck leaned forward with his hands on his knees to catch his breath. Then he looked sideways at Brihony.

'You see – underwater is safer!'

She gave a tired grin, still fighting to get her own breath back. 'Makes sense. You've got more chance of being attacked on the surface. They'll mistake you for a swimming animal. Underwater, they may decide you belong there and leave you alone.'

'Exactly,' grinned Beck. 'Even a croc expert can learn a new trick sometimes!'

'Well, that's one trick I never, ever intend to use again!' Brihony glanced across the river. 'What are those two drongoes doing now?'

The boat had reached the far bank and the men had pulled it onto the shore. Barega was passing boxes of kit to Ganan.

Beck felt in his pocket for his phone and held it up. The screen was dead and water trickled out of the case. He grimaced. So much for that form of communication. He walked carefully back to the river bank. Brihony followed close behind, keeping an eye out for anything that looked like a ripple or a floating log but wasn't.

Beck put his hands to his mouth and shouted, 'What's happening?'

His voice carried across the water and echoed back from the opposite cliff. The men came down to the water's edge so that Ganan could call back.

'Got a hole in the bow. We're not going anywhere until it's patched.'

'And it's all your own fault,' Brihony muttered quietly.

Beck saw no point in dwelling on who was to blame for the accident. 'How long?' he called back.

'We've got a repair kit. Says it takes twenty-four hours for the fibreglass to dry properly.'

'We're stuck here in the middle of Woop Woop for a *day*?' Brihony protested.

Beck sighed. There was no use fighting the inevitable. He called back for the last time. 'We'll make a camp over here. We'll climb up to higher ground, out of croc range. Talk to you in the morning.'

Brihony stared at him. 'Make a camp? What with? All the supplies were in the boat!'

He couldn't argue with that. He gave himself and Brihony a quick look over. His hat had come off in the accident – it would be floating down the river now. But he had his machete and water bottle. Brihony's hat had been kept on by a strap around her neck, so she still had that. Apart from these things and the clothes they were wearing, they had nothing.

He sighed. And he had so been looking forward to a proper holiday, in proper beds, eating proper food, and not having to survive anything. 'We can make do. Anyway, I thought you knew all about camping?' Beck smiled.

'Camping as in eating out of tins over a proper fire and sleeping in tents – why, sure!' Brihony replied.

'Well, this is almost the same. Only without the tins and tents.'

'And the fire?'

'Oh, the fire we can manage . . .'

'Gee, well, why didn't you say so?'

They climbed a narrow, sloping ridge of rock to the top of the bluff that overlooked the river. Dusk was drawing in and it was already almost too dark to see across now.

'You were right to want to call a halt,' Brihony admitted.

Beck just nodded as he looked about. A short way away a boab tree the size of a small house grew out of a small hollow in the rock. It had a thick, gnarly trunk many times wider than the spider-web of branches that grew out of the top. One of the branches had died and fallen off. Beck gave the tree a quick once-over. Unfortunately it didn't have any fruit or leaves, which would both have been edible. Baby boab roots made excellent food, but they would probably break their teeth on this one's roots.

So, no food. But between the base of the tree and the edges of the hollow, they would be out of the wind when they lay down.

'OK, here's our camp,' Beck said. He dug his heel into the ground to mark the spot. 'You hungry?'

'Not really. I had a bar just before the accident.'

'Yeah, me too.'

Brihony wrapped her arms around herself. 'Could

do with warming up, though. That fire you mentioned . . . ?'

'Coming right up.' It perfectly fitted in with Beck's own priorities. They would miss out on a proper dinner – the men had all the food – but neither of them would starve before morning, and he knew there would be plenty of food available if you knew where to look. Beck *did* know where to look, but he didn't want to go digging about in the dark. You had to see what you were digging. Australian snakes and spiders tended to be many times more poisonous than their cousins in the rest of the world.

Here in the Outback, animal life was scarce. A poisonous beastie wanted to be sure that once it had bitten its dinner, its dinner died promptly before it could get away.

Meanwhile, they were both still soaking wet, and the night would be getting cooler. So: food mattered less than fire right now.

Beck pointed at the fallen branch by the tree. 'Get what you can off that. Small twigs, bigger bits of wood – anything that will burn. Give everything a good kick or a knock before you lift it up. You don't know what else will be living in it, and could bite.'

'And then I'll come over to England,' Brihony said, 'and lecture you all about *English* wildlife. I have been camping once or twice before, Beck.'

'Sorry.' Beck grinned and passed her the machete. 'Use this. I'll get us some tinder.'

He did not have to look far in the fading light. From the boat he had already seen plenty of examples of what he was after: kapok bushes. They were taller than a man, but thin, so he could pull a trunk down to his level. The soft, furry leaves were shaped like maples – a cross between an outspread hand and the Ace of Spades. What he was after was nestled amongst them – the seed pods. They were like large nuts, oval and hard, the size of his hand. He gathered a bunch of them and carried them back to the camp in his shirt.

Brihony had made a small pile of wood. She had stripped the fallen branch as much as she could, and gathered other bits together as well. She had arranged the smaller pieces into a small tepee, and piled the larger pieces on top. That just left a space in the centre for what Beck had been fetching.

He spilled the pods out onto a piece of rock and knelt down. Brihony passed him the machete and, gripping it firmly, he brought the handle down hard on each one so that it split with a loud crack. Beck eased the tip of the blade into the opening and twisted so that the pod came apart.

Inside was the thing he was after. Each pod was packed full of fibres like stiff, dry cotton wool. Beck scooped them into a ball and packed it into the space at the heart of the tepee.

'So what do we do now?' Brihony asked. 'Rub sticks together?'

'That would be one way of doing it.' Beck took the fire steel from around his neck. 'Takes time, though.' He held the rod of ferrosium close to the fibre ball and scraped the square plate of steel along it. Bright, shining sparks streamed from the rod and fell onto the kapok.

A few more strikes and the fibre started smouldering. Tiny worms of glowing orange crept along each strand, consuming it as they did so. Beck put his face close to the fire and blew gently. The orange turned to yellow, then white, and spread throughout the ball. He poked more fibre in with a stick and watched as flames began to sprout from the gaps in the pile. Something went *crack* as moisture trapped in the wood turned to steam and burst out under its own pressure. That was the sound he always listened for: it told him that the fire had caught properly. The smell of wood smoke tickled his nostrils and a wavering heat brushed against his face.

'Or you can save a little time,' he told Brihony.

'Nice one, Beck!'

They huddled together by the fire, feeling their clothes begin to dry out and their spirits lift. They had taken their boots off and propped them up to face the fire. It was earlier than they would usually go to bed, but Beck knew they would wake up with the sun the next day. There were no curtains to keep it out for that extra couple of hours. And so they curled up on either side of the fire to get what rest they could.

Beck lay on his back with his hands behind his head and gazed up the sky. The skeletal, leafless branches of the boab tree above him weren't thick enough to block it out. 'Wow . . .' he murmured.

The sky was alive with a billion shining points of light – many, many more than he ever saw back in England. Al often told him how on a clear night, when he was younger, you could see the Milky Way even in an English sky. That was before the lights of towns and cities grew so bright that now only the brightest stars made their way through the light pollution.

But there was none of that here. The Milky Way was a clear band of stars as wide as his hand, stretching from horizon to horizon. There were other differences too. In the southern hemisphere, the constellations were different. It was not the first time Beck had seen the southern sky, but he always loved taking it all in. Here on the other side of the world, the man in the moon was standing on his head. One constellation, the Southern Cross, was so prominent it had made its way onto the flag of Australia. It lay low on the horizon, four key points of light with a slightly tilted cross-piece, surrounded by a cloud of smaller stars.

Finally Beck felt his eyes growing heavy and welcomed the wave of sleep that would shortly wash over him. His last waking thought was to wonder how Barega and Ganan were getting on . . .

Chapter 13

Something made Beck wake up. He lay staring at the smouldering embers of the fire. What had disturbed him? It wasn't discomfort. He was used to sleeping on the ground, and his clothes had just about dried out after their dunking.

He thought it might be dingoes, but they generally kept well away from humans. In the Kimberley there were always night-time noises, but nothing you could point to, and certainly nothing to jerk you out of sleep; just the sound of a vast and ancient land quietly getting on with its million-year-old business.

But then Beck heard it again, and he sat up. It was the sound of shouting voices.

He leaped nimbly to his feet and walked barefoot

to the edge of the hollow. His boots were still drying out by the fire and the ground was rough and dry beneath his soles. He carefully put his boots on and peered out into the dark, across the river. The entire gorge was one black ditch and he couldn't see anything. Then there was a flash of light – and another. Ganan and Barega had torches in their packs. Circles of light danced across the far bank, and one of them picked out a dark form that sent a shudder of recognition through Beck.

It only lasted for a second before the light moved on, but Beck had seen enough. The long, slow, armour-plated form of a crocodile moving silently over the river shore. The men must have camped close to the water.

'What is it?' Brihony had come to stand beside him.

'Croc near their camp.'

'Oh, no!'

The sound of shouting continued to drift across the water. Beck strained his ears to hear the words. 'Sounds like no one's been hurt.'

'How'd you make that out?'

'If they had been, they'd be screaming, not shouting.'

Brihony breathed out with relief. 'They'll probably be OK then. The croc's lost the element of surprise.'

'And that's their best weapon,' agreed Beck.

'Yep. Crocs like to feel in charge of the situation,' said Brihony. 'They're ambush hunters. They attack prey that can't fight back, or that didn't see them coming. The croc will probably leave them alone now it knows they've seen it.'

'You know that their jaws only have power in one direction, right?' Beck added.

'Yeah. A grown man can hold the jaws and stop them opening. Course, if they do open, then one bite could crush you.'

'And then you're a goner.' Beck took a final look into the darkness. 'Well, there's nothing we can do—'

Then he froze, because part of the darkness had shifted.

'*Move!*' he shouted. He helped Brihony on her way with a shove. She staggered backwards and then rounded on him, demanding to know what he was doing. But then she saw it too. First the jaws, then the rest of the saltwater crocodile as, metre by metre, it padded into their circle of firelight.

It must have come up the same rocky ridge they had used, Beck thought quickly. He would have thought that it was too steep. Maybe the croc had followed their scent, or maybe it was just curious, but either way, here it was.

They backed away in different directions, not taking their eyes off it. Its body snaked from side to side, the claws digging into the ground, looking like they could pierce steel. It seemed in no hurry, unable to decide which of them to aim for. Its body was broad – wider than it was high. It was low slung, though if it lifted its head up, it would be almost as tall as Beck. The armour plates along its back moved together as smoothly as if they had been turned out by a machine. Its mouth was shut, but snaggle teeth as long as Beck's fingers poked out where the jaws met.

OK . . . Beck ran through his options.

Fight it off with a piece of wood? He glanced quickly at the dead branch that still lay next to the fire. It was as thick as a man's leg, but too heavy to pick up and wield like a bat.

Hold its jaws closed? He didn't intend to get close enough to try that.

Beck had come face to face with bears and tigers. They had been angry, and had roared and snarled as if they wanted to punish him for intruding on their territory. He got nothing like that off the croc. It was completely calm, emotionless. He couldn't read its expression. It was born to eat, and they just happened to be juicy, tender mammals who would make a nice meal.

Where was the machete? he wondered. It was their only weapon, though even that would be pretty ineffective against an animal like this. Maybe he could aim the blade at its eyes. But though his machete was lying somewhere in their camp, he couldn't locate it without taking his eyes off the approaching saltie. That was something he had no intention of doing.

'Going to count to three,' he said, forcing his voice to be steady. 'When I get there, we both run behind that tree and climb it as quick as we can, right?'

'Ri . . .' Brihony's voice dried up and she had to try again. 'Right.'

'One, two—'

The crocodile lunged at Beck. He leaped to one side, over the fire, and hit the ground running. The croc's reflexes were faster than his, but Beck knew where he was headed. Right now the tree was their only hope of safety, and if he let the croc get between him and it, then he was dead.

The croc kept coming. Its body smashed into the fire, scattering the half-burned logs, and it writhed away from the hot embers.

Brihony was scrambling towards the boab, but the branches were too high for her to grab. Beck joined her and twined his fingers together into a cup, crouching so that she could put her foot into it.

'Quick!' They only had seconds. She stepped into his hands and he boosted her up as high as he could. In the same move he jumped behind the tree as the croc lunged forward again.

Now at least Beck had the boab between him and the croc, but sooner or later he would tire of dodging; this creature could move faster than him. And anyway, how did he know it was alone? Maybe the noise would attract others. He had to distract it so that he could join Brihony in the tree branches.

Branches . . . his eyes went to the fallen branch. Maybe he didn't need to actually fight the croc off with it – it had other uses. He began to sidle towards it, and the croc shifted on its front legs. Very slowly, Beck leaned down to get his hands under the branch . . .

The saltie attacked. There was no time to try and beat it off. Beck raised the branch over his head and threw it into the croc's open jaws.

The wood splintered as the croc clamped its mouth shut. Beck was already running for the tree, glimpsing the saltie's head thrashing from side to side. Having something – anything – in its mouth had triggered the instinct to twist and roll, to finish off its prey. It only took the killer a second to realize that it had been duped, but by then Beck had reached the tree. He leaped up, his feet trying to find some purchase on mottled trunk. Brihony leaned down, hand outstretched, feet braced against a branch to help her support his weight. She strained to pull him up, and he collapsed into a wooden hollow formed by the branches; he could have sworn he felt the gust of air as the croc's jaws snapped shut where his foot had just been.

Chapter 14

It was a long hard night. The crook of the branches was just big enough to accommodate the two of them, but it was mighty uncomfortable and it was impossible to stretch out to sleep. If they dozed off, heads nodding forward, they would suddenly jerk awake with the horrible feeling that they were falling.

But dawn came eventually. The shapes of hills and gorges grew solid out of the dark as the rosy light slid over the Kimberley. Beck peered down into their camp.

The fire had gone out, destroyed by the croc's charge – just a dark smudge of ash on the red soil, surrounded by charred sticks. There was no sign of the croc.

They climbed down, cautious, neither of them

daring to hope that it had really gone. Beck surveyed the camp quickly. There was the machete, still propped against the trunk of the tree where he had left it. He looked around for the water bottle, so vital to their survival. There it was, over to one side. Its presence was almost as welcome as the absence of crocodile.

He was about to wave the bottle triumphantly to show Brihony when he saw the desolation on her face. She looked on the verge of tears.

'I'm sorry, Beck.'

'What about?' he asked in surprise.

'I . . . I thought we were far enough from the river. We should have been safe. Mum would have known . . . if she was with us . . .'

Beck realized he had barely given Mia Stewart a thought since the previous day; whereas Brihony must be thinking of her constantly.

'Hey, it wasn't your fault!' he hastened to reassure her. 'You were right about them being ambush hunters, weren't you? It went away because it realized it was too far out of its comfort zone and had lost the element of surprise.'

'It took its time to work that out,' she said with feeling.

'The main thing is, it's gone. We should see how the others did.'

Beck quickly checked Brihony's boots, holding them upside down and shaking hard to get rid of any Australian wildlife that had taken up residence during the night – scorpions or spiders that had mistaken them for a nice, cool, dark cave to hide up in during the hours of daylight. Then they walked to the edge of the hollow. The scene looked calm and tranquil, with the wide river flowing on as it always had. The boat was pulled up on the far shore, but there was no sign of Barega or Ganan. His heart pounded. *Please don't let the crocs have got them. Please . . .*

Then his eyes narrowed as he peered across. From the top of the bluffs on the far side of the gorge he could just make out a thin trickle of smoke. He cupped his hands to his mouth and drew breath into his lungs to shout. 'Hello? Ganan? Barega? You there?'

The sound echoed up and down the river. It faded away into silence, and then there was movement.

Two human figures appeared. Relief flowed over Beck like cool water on a hot day.

'Beck? Is that you?' It was Barega calling.

Brihony came to stand beside Beck. 'No, it's Her Majesty the Queen and the Governor General,' she muttered.

Beck grinned. 'How did you sleep?' he called.

'Not great.' Barega didn't know that Beck was fully aware of what had happened during the night, so it was quite an understatement. 'You need to watch out. There's crocs about.'

'Gee, thanks,' Beck called back. 'We'll keep our eyes open.' Brihony laughed.

'Sorry we can't bring you any breakfast,' Barega continued.

Breakfast! Beck realized that he really was hungry now. It was a long time since they'd eaten their fruit bars, and the excitement of the night had burned energy. They needed food.

'Never mind,' he shouted. 'Talk to you later.'

They went back to the camp and Beck picked up the water bottle. It was almost empty, and unfortunately there was only one source of water nearby.

'The crocs better let me refill the bottle?' he mused.

'Make sure you walk along the beach a bit to do it,' Brihony replied. 'Get away from the point where we came ashore last night. Crocs have good memories, and if they see an animal come to a particular place to drink, that's where they'll wait next time.'

'Yep. Keep a watch from up here,' he said.

He made his way cautiously down the rocky ledge to the shore, eyes peeled for any disturbance in the water, and carried on for twenty metres before stopping. The water bubbled as the bottle filled with a series of glugs. He screwed the top on and hurried back along the path to the top of the cliff. Then he paused and his eyes lit up.

'What is it?' Brihony called down from above.

'I just saw breakfast! Keep watching for crocs.'

He hadn't noticed it the previous night, but a tall thin tree clung to the side of the rocky cliff. Its trunk was skinny and twisted, its bark a lifeless grey, the colour of old ashes. It was a rock fig tree – and rock figs were good energy.

Beck climbed the first couple of metres. The roots of the tree dug into the cliff side and made good holds for his hands and feet. He came to the first of the leaves. They were oval, and covered in a light coating of fur to keep the moisture in. He poked his fingers into the clusters of leaves and found what he was after. The yellow fruits were the size of apricots, growing in little knots, protected by the leaves. They felt firm when he gave them an experimental squeeze. He plucked as many as he could reach, and stuffed them into his pockets. Then, with a final check of the shore, he climbed back down and hurried up the cliff to join Brihony.

When he reached the top, he took a look over the Outback. The vista of green plainland and red rock was already starting to shimmer in the sun's heat. He was glad for what little shade the boab provided. He remembered that he had lost his hat the day before. If they had to move out of the shade, then he would have to deal with that.

But meanwhile he would see if he could add to the breakfast larder. While Brihony rebuilt the fire, he started to look around for anything else that might go with the figs. Now that it was daylight he felt safer poking about.

He used the machete to lever rocks up. The first yielded a large spider. It waved its slender brown legs in indignation at the disturbance. Beck was going nowhere near any Australian spiders, so he flicked it away.

Next he found something very long and spiny, with many legs and far too many hairs. It trundled over the ground, its middle flowing over obstacles while its front and back kept walking straight. Again he thought, *No thanks*. Long hairs on a creature like this were defensive – they got into an attacker's skin, and at the very least could itch unbearably. They might even be poisonous. It might be OK if he cooked it to remove the hairs, but it wasn't worth the risk.

The branch that had saved him from the croc the previous night had been bitten in two, but it could still do him another favour. He levered up the bark with the tip of the machete, and a curling, writhing grub fell into his hands. It was about the size of his little finger. Now, that was more like it. With a bit more exploring of the soft inner wood, he pushed the number up to six.

'Huhu grubs! You tried them before?' he asked cheerfully. He held them out for Brihony to see.

She frowned. 'No. But my mum has once.'

It was like a cold wind had suddenly blown over Beck's cheerfulness. They still only had the doctor's word for it that Mia would be OK. Brihony was probably thinking of her mum a lot more than she let on.

'Well, they're breakfast,' he said, trying to remain optimistic. They were stuck in the middle of the Outback. The one thing no one could afford to do was get depressed about their situation, or worry about things they couldn't solve. They had to stay positive. *Stay cheerful in adversity*, Beck's dad had often told him.

Brihony's face froze, then slowly screwed up. 'Breakfast? As in, first meal of the day?'

'That's the only breakfast I know,' he told her, grinning.

She slowly looked up at him with eyes that begged him to give the right answer. 'You are kidding? Please?'

He had to smile at her expression. 'You mean, in all your previous camping you never tried these?'

'Well, gee, what were we thinking? I mean, eating out of proper tins with proper hot food in them when we could have had *bugs*?'

'Well, I can do the proper hot food bit. Unless you'd prefer them cold.'

'Hot,' she said decisively. 'Take my mind off what I'm actually eating.'

And so Beck used the machete to sharpen the end of a stick, and they skewered the grubs and held them over a flame. They had to judge it right – too close and they would turn to cinders, which was no good to anyone. Beck knew from experience that if you ate them cold, they tasted of nothing on the outside and cold snot inside. At least cooking warmed them up and you could almost imagine they were mini sausages. Almost.

In between the grubs they feasted on the rock figs, which were almost as unappetizing. The fruit split open to reveal a red cavity lined with hundreds of seeds. There was plenty to sink your teeth into, but it tasted and felt like they were chewing on old cardboard.

They washed the meal down with swigs of water from the bottle, after carefully boiling it first. It was the first time on this trip that they had drunk water from the river rather than a tap or a bottled source. It felt softer in their mouths, with a tang that made them smack their lips.

'May I just say . . .' Brihony hiccupped. 'That was the most disgusting meal I have ever—'

She stopped and stared at Beck as, out of nowhere, a noise filled the air.

It was a sound that no machine could make – but it wasn't an animal either; a bass drone like a cross between a cloud of angry insects and the thrumming of bicycle wheels on a pavement. It seemed to vibrate out of the ground itself, and rose and fell and rose again as it echoed across the Outback.

'What the heck is that?'

'Bullroarer!' Beck exclaimed. He leaped to his feet. It took him a moment, and then he had it. 'There, see?'

A few kilometres in the distance, away from the

river, a red sandstone bluff rose up out of the shimmering plain. At the top was a black dot. It was a human figure, and it seemed to be waving one arm. Something whirled around its head like a circling bird.

'Back when he was training me, Pindari always used a bullroarer to summon me. I think it's him!'

Chapter 15

The noise died away. Beck blinked, and the figure was gone. He glared at where it had been.

'Do you think it really was Pindari?' Brihony asked.

'I couldn't say . . . but who else would be using a bullroarer in the middle of nowhere?'

'Hmm. How about – well – anyone?'

Beck smiled. She had a point.

There was no sound on earth quite like a bull-roarer. The one thing it did *not* sound like was a bull roaring. You spun a shaped piece of wood around your head on a piece of twisted cord. This made the wood rotate, and as it cut through the air it produced that sound. It was thousands of years old, used by ancient peoples all over the globe to send messages across long distances. And Pindari had been a master.

'Put it this way. Even if it wasn't Pindari, no one uses those things just for fun. They're meant to communicate Someone was trying to communicate with us. Get our attention.'

'OK,' Brihony agreed. 'That bit worked. Now what?'

'Well, he wouldn't just be saying "Yoo-hoo, here I am." If he was saying anything, it would be "Come to me."'

Beck wasn't quite sure he dared to believe his own logic. But deep down in his bones, he knew that the man *had* been Pindari.

They stared across the plain. The man had been so close. On straight, level ground, Beck could run that distance in a few minutes. But it was anything but straight and level, and there were all manner of obstacles in between.

'Or he could come to us . . .' Brihony murmured.

'But then, why announce it? Why not just turn up?'

'Maybe we should go and ask him . . .?' she suggested, her voice trailing off into a question.

Beck considered. It was more exciting than staying put until the evening, which had been the original plan. On the other hand, they had hardly any supplies or equipment. If they stayed where they were, they would expend less energy, and be in less danger. In any survival situation, staying put and waiting for rescue was usually the best idea. You needed a powerful reason to move off.

But he *had* a powerful reason. He had been brought here to track down Pindari, and the Jungun tribe needed what Pindari had. They might not get another chance like this. He couldn't let it pass.

'Maybe we should,' he agreed. He stood up and ran through all the options in his mind. What could go wrong?

Answer: a lot, he thought grimly.

They had no food. Well, he knew how to find that.

They had no protection; but at least they were dressed for the Outback and he knew how to look after himself.

But the biggest risk was always dehydration. The hotter and more humid the place, the greater the risk. Lack of water could kill you in a matter of hours, and they only had one water bottle between them.

Dehydration was more than just being thirsty. With severe dehydration you actually stopped feeling thirsty. Meanwhile your heart would beat overtime, you would grow delirious and ultimately you would die. But before that, your body would just start packing in. Your muscles would lose their strength; your ability to concentrate would vanish; you might be unable to find help simply because your mind and body were too far gone.

Answer: don't let it get to that stage. The water bottle held five litres, and Beck knew they could get to that bluff and back on two and a half each. And if they had to go further, thanks to Pindari, Beck knew other ways to get water.

'So . . . ?' Brihony asked, watching him standing there, apparently doing nothing.

'So. We need to know where we're going.'

She pointed at the bluff where the figure had been. 'That way?'

'Yeah, but which way is that?' The bluff was quite prominent, but apart from that there was nothing to distinguish it from any other mound of rock. If they started moving towards it, it could very easily get lost in the landscape. Beck scraped his heel into the ground, digging a straight line that pointed to where the man had been. That would help them tell it apart, at least from where they stood. Then he raised his left wrist and angled his watch, squinting across the face towards the sun.

'Whatcha doin'?'

'Southern hemisphere navigation.' He was glad his watch had survived the river, even if his phone had not. It was certified to a hundred metres – it could handle a bit of wet. 'Point twelve o'clock at the sun. Halfway between that and the hour hand is north. Northern hemisphere, other way round – point the hour hand at the sun. So, north is' – he gestured with a chop of his hand – 'that way. Means we're heading . . .'

'North-east,' Brihony finished, looking at the angle between the direction Beck had indicated and the line he had drawn in the ground. 'Almost exactly.'

'Cool.'

Ganan and Barega sounded less pleased when Beck called across the river to them.

'Great,' Ganan shouted back. 'So how do we follow you?'

'We might be back by this evening,' Beck told him. 'But in case we're not, I've left a mark on the ground, showing the direction. And I'll leave a trail for you to follow along the way.'

'How long are you planning on being gone?' Brihony asked in surprise. 'He wasn't that far away.'

'He wasn't far away when we saw him,' Beck corrected. 'If that was Pindari and he's moving about, then we just don't know, do we? Or he might take us to wherever he's put the memory stick.'

He could see from her thoughtful expression that she hadn't considered that.

The two men were conversing; then they heard Ganan's voice again.

'I really don't like you going off on your own.'

'I can handle it! This is why you wanted me, remember?'

And I'm going anyway, Beck added silently. His mind was made up; he wasn't asking permission. Finding Pindari could help the Jungun, it could help him learn more about his parents' death, and it would help Brihony find justice for the people who'd hurt her mother. Everyone would get something out of this except Lumos, and that was just fine by him.

Still, he would rather go with Barega and Ganan's blessing, rather than defying them.

Finally the answer came.

'OK. If you come back today, then great. If not, we'll follow you as best we can. If we lose you, we'll just head back to this spot and wait. We're trusting you a heck of a lot, Beck.'

No, Beck thought, *you're trusting Pindari, who trusted me*.

But all he called back was: 'See you later.'

He and Brihony went back down to the river, taking care once again to go to a different part of the shoreline, so they could each drink as much water as possible.

'Best place to carry it,' Beck said. 'Inside you.'

They filled the bottle one last time and hurried back up to the camp. A full five-litre bottle is heavy, and Beck wasn't looking forward to lugging it across the Outback, but he knew there was no choice – and besides, it would get lighter every time they drank from it.

He was also mighty glad to be moving away from the river. There were plenty of other dangerous creatures out there, but salties were the ones most likely to attack without warning.

There was one more thing to take care of, though Beck had been putting it off. He gazed out across the Outback one last time. The day had warmed up. In the shade of the boab's thick trunk, it was merely hot. Out there, the sun hit down like a hammer.

'I, uh . . .' he began.

Brihony looked surprised at hearing the sudden hesitation in his voice.

'I, uh . . . need you to – to look the other way for a moment.'

'What for?'

'Because I, uh – I need to . . . take my trousers off.'

She paused, then a disbelieving smile spread over her face. 'Beck, I have seen boys in their dacks before.'

'Yes, but, I – uh, I – uh . . . I need to take them off too.'

The smile vanished. 'OK . . . Look, Beck, if you want to go, then . . .'

'Just . . . look away? Please?'

She sighed and turned round. 'Carry on, in your own time . . .'

After a short while he said, 'OK, done.'

She turned round to see Beck with his trousers on again, solemnly placing his shorts over his head. He knotted the elastic waistband to hold them on.

Brihony let out a peal of astonished, disbelieving laughter. '*What*? Oh, that's *disgusting*! Beck, you've been wearing those for over twenty-four hours . . .'

'Yeah, and don't I know it.' His face creased into a smile. 'But I lost my hat in the river, and that sun could literally fry my brains. I'd use my shirt, but then I'd die of sunburn. So I don't have a lot of choice.'

'I suppose they're quite cute, in a weird sort of way.' Brihony peered more closely. 'Stripes are OK. At least you don't have cartoon animals or anything . . .'

'OK, OK,' Beck said gruffly. He took one last look around the camp. The empty kapok seed pods still lay close by. He picked up a couple thoughtfully, and cupped them in his hand. Then he pushed one into his pocket and handed the other to Brihony. 'You might need this.'

'What for?'

'Um . . .' He really didn't want to tell her. 'I only said you *might*. If you do, I'll let you know, right?'

She frowned, but took it. 'OK . . .'

They were ready to go. As a final act Beck kicked sand and earth across the fire to extinguish it. A rogue spark in the bone-dry Outback could start a blaze that would sweep across miles of open land.

There wasn't any more they could do here.

'Right,' Beck said. 'Let's get tracking.'

Chapter 16

Going out in the daytime, Beck thought. *I must be mad . . .*

Walking into the Outback was like walking into an oven. The air was so hot, he felt he was pushing his way through it. Normally he would never travel like this. In the desert you travelled when the sun was low; or preferably at night, when it wasn't there. While it was high in the sky, slowly grilling everything beneath it, you took shelter and slept.

In this case, that was not an option. Unlike the desert, the terrain here was rugged. There was too much to trip over in the dark; and besides, the man they were after was moving during the day. So they had to as well.

Walking away from the river, they were heading

across a plain of scrubland. Here and there in the distance, small hills and cliffs of red sandstone punched up out of the ground. The Kimberley wasn't a desert like the Sahara, an endless ocean of sand. There was plenty of vegetation. From a distance the shrubs and bushes looked like they grew thick and close together. In fact, there was plenty of space between them, and very few of them came higher than Beck's waist. The trees were few and far between, but even so it meant they could pause in the shade for a few minutes, and take a mouthful of water.

Beck kept his eyes on the distant bluff that was their destination, and was very glad they had taken a bearing on it first. As he suspected, it changed as their perspective moved. After ten minutes of walking, he could not have distinguished it from any other outcroppings of red rock without some help. Every time they stopped, Beck took another bearing off the sun to work out which way they ought to be heading. Then he would make another mark in the ground for the men to find, if they followed.

He knew it would be very easy to drift off course.

They might walk round a tall rock or a cluster of bushes – just enough to make them lose their orientation by a small fraction. But as they continued in the new direction, that small fraction would grow larger and larger, and they could end up missing their destination by a mile. Staying on track was critical.

Beck kept his eyes peeled for any signs of human life. As far as they knew, the man hadn't come any closer than the bluff. That would be their starting point. For now, all they had to do was get there.

The ground was firm beneath their feet. It was dry earth and rock, easy to walk on. It was still morning, so the sun was climbing as they walked and the Outback was getting hotter. They set a steady pace, not talking any more than they had to. The last thing Beck had said before leaving the camp was: 'Breathe through your nose, not your mouth. There's moisture in your breath and you lose it more quickly through your mouth.'

That had been half an hour ago. Now he suddenly held up his hand and stopped.

'What is it?' Brihony asked.

Her face was shaded by her bush hat, and Beck felt a stab of jealousy. His shorts were doing their job on his head – they helped protect him from the full force of the sun eating into his brains. But his face was still exposed and he knew he must be dripping with sweat. But he smiled. 'I just saw elevenses . . .'

It was a low, wide shrub that was tangled up with at least one other bush. The leathery green leaves were long, slender and pointed, and grew in pairs along the branches. Fruit grew in the shape of hard, red, waxy spheres the size of billiard balls. Beck plucked one and handed it to Brihony.

'Quandong?' she guessed. 'I've only had this out of tins.'

'Well, this is better— Wait!'

Brihony had sunk her teeth into it. Her face contorted and she gave a muffled yelp of pain. 'Ow!'

'It's a kind of peach,' Beck finished. Brihony had just learned this the hard way. The fruit contained a massive stone – the flesh was only about half a centimetre deep. 'You OK?'

'Almost lost a tooth . . .' she muttered, but she nibbled and sucked at the remaining flesh while

Beck picked one for himself. The fruit was juicy, which gave them a little more liquid, and he knew it was high in Vitamin C. According to Pindari, it was essential food for any traveller.

They filled their pockets with as many quandongs as they could carry. Beck took another bearing and they set off again.

He felt his heart lifting as they walked. How could it not? People who didn't know anything looked at the Outback and saw a harsh, hostile land. Far too hot in the dry season, far too wet in the wet season, and filled with too many creatures that could kill you.

But Beck and Brihony, and people like them, saw a land full of plants and wildlife that were perfectly adapted to their environment. A land of balance. There was give and there was take. It was complex and beautiful, and it deserved respect, not fear. Beck had been told that the first Aboriginal people came to Australia about 45,000 years ago. He always reckoned that if they hadn't seen something worthwhile, they would have just turned round and gone away again. No one made them stay. They remained because they recognized the promise and the beauty of this mighty land.

They came to the edge of a gorge that cut through the sandstone at their feet. It was a dry river bed, six or seven metres deep. The bottom was lined with smooth stones and bushes that grew among them. No water had flowed down it for a long time, though Beck had seen what could happen when it rained in the Outback. A flash flood. Water would come cascading down, and the dry bed of stones would be a raging torrent within minutes. Too many people had been killed that way.

Instinctively he looked up at the sky, but there was no sign of rain clouds. He turned his head and squinted along the course of the bed. He knew that flash floods could strike many miles from where it had actually rained.

If he remembered the map correctly – the one he had studied on the boat – the river curved north ahead of where they'd had their accident. This dry river bed probably ran into it. There was no point in walking along it – that would just take them way off course; they would have to cross it.

The sides were steep but not vertical, and Beck could see plenty of nooks and crannies for foot- and handholds.

He made another mark at the point where the ground dropped away. 'You up for some climbing?' he asked.

'No worries,' Brihony told him.

They climbed down side by side, so that neither of them would dislodge rocks that might fall on the other. They moved carefully. The sandstone had a strange feel to it, almost greasy, and it flaked away if you held it too tight. It was an unpleasant feeling to be suspended over a sheer drop, holding onto the rock, and feeling it crumble away beneath your fingers.

Beck reached the bottom before Brihony. He looked up to check her progress. She was still halfway down, arms and legs stretched out to hold herself.

'How are you doing?' he called.

Very slowly she wiggled a foot across the rock face into a new crevice. Just as slowly, she moved a hand. 'How does it look?' Her voice shook slightly.

'Just move one limb at a time. You've got four points of contact holding you up – two feet, two hands. Keep three of them steady at all times and just move one—'

'I know that, Beck Granger, thank you very much!' she snapped. 'Got any handy clues for people who just happen to *hate heights*?'

' "Don't look down" always helps,' Beck replied teasingly.

'Yeah, thank you again, Beck . . .' Painstakingly, Brihony shifted one hand a little lower. 'I don't mind being high and looking down. Cliffs, tall buildings, aeroplanes – all fine. But I *hate* not having anything under me . . .'

'You've got plenty under you.' Beck spied out the cracks and ledges beneath her. In his mind's eye he could map her way down as if it was a ladder painted on the side of the cliff. 'Move your left foot five centimetres to the left . . . Yup, like that . . .'

With his guidance, Brihony could move a little faster, and she picked up more speed as her confidence grew. Another minute and she was down on the ground with Beck.

'No worries!' She beamed brightly and flexed her arms. 'But give it a couple of minutes before we climb up again. My arms are killing me.'

He smiled, and held his hands out at shoulder height. 'Try not to put your arms any higher than this when you climb. It's the same level as your heart, more or less. If you stretch them higher than that, the blood drains out of them, your heart has to work harder, your muscles ache and you get tired more quickly.'

'Got it,' she said as they picked their way across the river bed into the shade of the gorge's northern face. She swung her arms in circles a few times to loosen them up. 'OK, ready for part two now.'

They had another quandong each, and more water, and turned towards the rock face they had to climb. Beck made another mark with his heel to show the spot.

Brihony reached out with her hands, then let them drop to her side again. 'Oh, jeez.'

Beck glanced at her sideways. 'You really don't like heights, do you?'

She shook her head. 'Hate 'em. It's not having

anything beneath you that does it. And not being able to see where you're going. Not properly.'

'Why don't I guide you again?' he offered. 'I'll wait down here at the bottom, and I'll tell you where to put your feet and hands.'

She looked at him gratefully. 'Would you? Thanks.'

'Well, then, up you go. Put your hands there and there . . .'

He stepped back to get a better view as she started to climb. As before, his mind created a ladder above her – he could see exactly where she should put her hands and feet. None of the holds were more than a metre apart; she never had to stretch far.

This side of the gorge was higher than the one they had climbed down – ten metres or more by Beck's reckoning.

'Now,' he called when Brihony was halfway up. 'Just above your head, to the left, there's a kind of ledge. You can have a rest there if you like.'

''Kay.' Her voice was muffled by the rock only centimetres from her face. She reached out a hand towards the ledge, shifted her body over a little . . . and stopped.

She stayed there, unmoving, and didn't say anything.

Beck gazed up at her, puzzled. 'What's up?'

'Beck . . .' Her voice shook. 'We've got company. Up here.' Her tone said it was not the kind of company they were after.

'What is it?'

'Beck, it's a king brown, and it's here in front of me – it's looking right at me.'

Beck's heart thudded. Translated, what Brihony had just said was that one of the most poisonous snakes in the world was only centimetres from her outstretched hand.

Chapter 17

'Don't move,' Beck called. 'I'm coming up.'

He began to scramble up the crumbling wall of rock, as quickly as he dared.

Beck had already been through the options in his head. The snake hadn't attacked Brihony – yet. There was no particular reason to think it would, if it didn't feel threatened. But she couldn't even withdraw her hand, in case it mistook the movement for some kind of threat. She couldn't climb back down – not with a venomous snake literally hanging over her head. And she certainly couldn't keep climbing. Even if she was only passing through, the king brown could give her a bite that could kill her very fast. The dose of neurotoxin injected straight into her bloodstream would start its work almost immediately, attacking the nerves that controlled all her movements – including her breathing and the beating of her heart. She would die fighting for breath, heart pounding out of control, paralysed and in pain.

It took him only a minute to reach the ledge, a short distance from where Brihony was. He looked along it at her pale face, and at the snake in between.

It was at least two metres long, with a body as thick as a man's arm. Its tail was still concealed in a dark crack in the rock. It must have been sleeping in there when it heard Brihony coming. Maybe it had mistaken the vibrations for something more its own size – a lizard, or a small mammal. Maybe even a dingo with unusual rock-climbing skills. And so it had come out to investigate.

The dark-rimmed scales were like brown leather. It looked like someone had just dumped a mass of scaly coils onto the ledge. The blunt head was raised, the eyes, like small black pebbles, aimed squarely at Brihony's face. The snake flicked its tongue, sampling the air.

It adjusted its position slightly. Glistening, smooth scales slid over one another as it tightened its coils.

Beck had held many snakes before and he knew what they felt like. They weren't at all slimy, but dry, like polished leather coated in smooth wax.

The snake hadn't yet noticed Beck come up further along the ledge. Beck swallowed. What he was about to do was risky and could get at least one of them killed. But he had no other option. He had to kill the snake before either it struck out at Brihony, or Brihony's arms and legs gave way and she fell eight metres to the rocky ground. Both could end up being fatal.

If he'd had the luxury of doing this on flat ground, he would have done it differently. He would have found a long stick with a bend at the end, and used it to pin down the snake's head from a safe distance. Then Brihony could have moved past it safely.

Halfway up a rock face and with no stick, that wasn't possible. And so he pulled out the machete, made sure his grip was secure, and breathed deeply.

'Beck,' Brihony whispered. 'Be careful, but hurry. I can't hold on much longer.'

He didn't answer, his eyes fixed on the snake in front of him. He deliberately reached out with the machete towards the king brown.

In a flash of movement, the serpent struck out at the steel blade and its bare fangs clashed against the metal. The snake's tiny brain couldn't process the fact that the machete wasn't part of Beck.

Before it could figure out its mistake, Beck slashed at a point just behind its head. Some snakes have quite thin necks between head and body; the neck of a king brown is exactly as thick and muscular as the rest of it, so Beck put all his strength into the single-handed machete blow. The blade rang out as it hit rock, drowning out the dull thud as it passed through the snake's body. The head lay severed from the twitching coils, and the jaw opened and closed as though it was delivering a final dying curse.

Beck used the tip of the blade to flick the head away from Brihony and him. Better safe than sorry – even a severed snake's head could deliver venom.

Brihony sagged against the rock face in relief. Beck grinned across at her.

'Can you keep climbing?'

She nodded silently, and started off again, moving nervously past the twitching body of the dead snake.

Beck then shuffled along the ledge and picked up the body, draping it round his neck. The tail end slid limply out of the crack it had emerged from. He resisted the urge to inspect the opening. Maybe there was another snake in there. Maybe it had laid eggs. Eggs would be good eating under many circumstances, but not now. As far as the Aboriginal peoples were concerned, the Outback owned them, not vice versa. Beck had no need to kill unborn snakes that presented no threat to him.

And so he kept climbing, with the dead snake hanging round his shoulders like a grisly scarf.

Brihony was sitting on the ground at the top, legs drawn up so she could hug her knees. Colour was returning to her face but she grimaced when she saw him. 'That gives me the creeps, Beck.'

Beck smiled. 'Good energy, though.' He held up the severed end and let it drop again. 'Lean protein. Low fat and easy to digest. Meet our supper!'

She pulled a face. 'You're not going to carry that around all day!'

'No, and I don't need to,' he said gratefully. He turned to what he was pretty sure was their destination, and took another direction reading with the sun. Sure enough, it was almost due north-east. 'We're almost where we saw the guy. We'll stop and cook the meat there, in the shade.'

'I thought you shouldn't eat too much when you're low on water. It just uses moisture digesting it.'

He looked at her with respect. 'You're right, but we won't eat much now,' he said. 'We'll cook it and carry it with us to eat this evening. But we don't want to be moving about in the midday heat. We'll carry on searching when the day starts to cool down again. That's assuming Pindari's not just sitting waiting for us anyway.' He held out a hand. 'Coming?'

Brihony let him pull her to her feet, and they set off on the final stretch.

The bluff they had been heading for was gently rounded and they simply walked to the top, their boots gripping the bare rock.

There was no one there. Whoever it was they had seen with the bullroarer, that person was gone.

Beck shrugged the snake off his shoulders, leaving it lying in the shade of a bush. He stood with his hands on his hips, gazing out across the scrubland, eyes peeled for anything that might be another human being. He was just looking at more Outback. Miles and miles and miles, reaching out to the horizon in all directions. The air shook and shifted in the heat; it would have been hard to focus on anything smaller than a tree.

If there was someone out there, he would have to be tracked the old-fashioned way.

'So where to now?' Brihony asked.

'First, water.' Beck handed over the bottle and they each took another swig. 'And then we start looking. This is definitely the place. We need to find his tracks.'

'So we just look at the ground?'

'It's not just footprints. There could be signs in the vegetation – leaves bent towards the way he went . . . things like that – but yes, looking at the ground is a good place to start. Watch very carefully where you put your own feet.' He looked around to get his bearings. 'Right. You go and stand by that bush there, at the edge of the rock. And I' – he raised his voice to call across to her as he headed for a bush on the other side – 'will go over here. OK. Now, you walk slowly towards that tree over there – you see the one?'

'Uh-huh.' The tree he was pointing at was about thirty metres away, dead ahead of Brihony.

'Walk over there, keeping your eye on the ground for any footprints that aren't ours. When you get there, turn round, take a step to your right, and come back to the edge here. And I'll make for that bush there, then I'll take a step to my left, so . . .'

'Bit by bit we'll search every square metre of the ground.' She nodded to show she understood. 'I've got it.'

'Let's do it!'

Beck had spent several weeks with Pindari. The first week and a bit had just been failure after failure, because he hadn't learned to concentrate. But in the end he had got the feel for it.

All other thoughts had to go to the back of your mind: what you were going to eat next; did you want to go to the toilet; what were they doing back home; even the harmless little tune you wanted to whistle – it all had to go. Tracking required total concentration and great stamina. If you watched nothing but dry earth scroll past your eyes for five minutes, the temptation was to start taking short cuts and jumping ahead. You looked over the next bit of ground quickly because you assumed it would be just the same – but that could be where the clue lay. Every square centimetre of ground had to get the same level of concentration, and that level had to be one hundred per cent.

It was enough to make your brain overheat and your eyes sting in a very short time.

And it was Brihony who found the first trace, ten minutes later. She waved him over. 'Ta-dah!'

Beck looked at what she had found. A shallow depression in the rock was filled with red earth. In the centre was a single footprint. Whoever made it had been barefoot: the five toes were clearly visible. It was stamped into the earth, the sole broad, the toes massive – someone who had never worn shoes but had spent decades walking about the Outback on feet that were as tough as leather.

'So . . .' Beck said. 'Where are the rest? Was he hopping?'

Brihony frowned and looked about her. The earth around the footprint was completely clear of any other disturbance for at least a metre in all directions.

'That's nuts!' she exclaimed. 'He must have really tried hard to leave just one print. What's his game?'

Beck squinted thoughtfully. They still didn't know for sure that it was Pindari they had seen. But if it was, he was pretty sure he knew what would be going through Pindari's mind.

'I think it's a test,' he said. 'It's his way of saying, "If you want to find me – start here." '

Chapter 18

The thought that Pindari might be close made Beck's heart pound. He could tell that Brihony felt the same way. They both wanted to go and find him *now*.

But it was noontime in the Kimberley, the heat was merciless, and Beck was uncomfortably aware of their water situation. He held the bottle up to the light to check its contents. It was still over half full – they were OK for water for the time being. But they wouldn't be going straight back to the river. From now on, water was a precious resource and had to be conserved. And that meant they had to sit out the hottest part of the day or they would just end up as food for the dingoes.

So they made a temporary camp in the shade of a eucalyptus tree a short distance away from the footprint. The shade wasn't much – the leaves hung vertically, letting some sun through – but it was enough to keep the worst off. Brihony built a fire and used Beck's fire steel to light it, while Beck set to work on the snake.

First he made a shallow incision at the tail end with the machete. He sliced his way up the snake's belly to where its head had been, then put down the machete and worked his finger under the skin by the severed neck. After that it was easy to peel it back. He held the neck with one hand and the skin with the other, and slowly stripped it away as if peeling a banana. He cut it off at the end, where he had made his first cut. The skin was now completely separate from the carcass.

Last of all Beck needed to remove the guts. He made another slit along the belly, this time into the flesh. The snake's innards were conveniently arranged in a tight roll, so he just had to work his finger around it and pull. Out came a glistening, grey-blue mass almost as long as the body itself.

'That is the most disgusting thing I have ever seen,' Brihony declared.

'More disgusting than a boy wearing his undies on his head?'

'Nah, that's just weird.' She looked at the skinned snake. 'This is going to be delicious!'

'It will be, when we eat it,' he reminded her. 'Which isn't now.'

'Oh. Yeah. That whole dehydration thing . . .'

Brihony wound the gutted carcass around a stick to hold over the fire, while Beck dumped the skin and guts a good distance away from the camp. They would attract ants anyway, so they might as well do so far from any humans they might want to bite.

Then they sat with their backs to the tree, cooking the snake and enjoying the shade.

'Aren't we taking it a little too easy?' Brihony asked. 'The guy could be miles away by now.'

'He *will* be miles away by now,' Beck corrected her.

'OK, even more miles.'

'We're following footprints, and the best way to see prints is when the light comes at them from a low angle. It casts shadows so that the print stands out more. At noon, when the sun is right on top of us, the light shines straight down and the shadows disappear. So do the footprints.'

'So the best times for tracking would be early morning or late afternoon?'

'Exactly. But we won't wait till late afternoon or it'll be dark before we get anywhere. We'll give it another hour.'

An hour later they were ready. Beck allowed them a single piece of snake meat each. It had almost no taste apart from the smoke of the fire. It was stringy, light and quite chewy, and it had almost no fat on it.

Then they cut into strips as much as they could carry in their pockets for later, and reluctantly left the rest behind.

Then they went back to the single footprint they had found – the one that Beck had said meant *Start here*. Beck logically started to look in the direction that the footprint was pointing. There was nothing for a few metres, but then he came across another print. The ground was too hard for a regular trail, but soon after that, he found another. And then another.

After that, nothing. By the time Beck had gone

another ten metres he was pretty certain he had lost the trail.

He went back to Brihony. She saw from his face that he was already feeling annoyed with himself.

'Can I do anything?' she asked.

'Stand there.' He pointed at the last footprint he had seen. 'You need to follow and stand by every trace I find. That way, if I lose the trail, I can always come back to the last point I had it.'

'Got it.'

From that last footprint, the man could have gone in three possible directions. There was a pair of scrub bushes ahead. Beck had assumed he had gone on between them. However, he might have gone left or he might have gone right. Beck tried the left track first, and almost immediately got lucky. There were two footprints in quick succession.

Something was bothering him and he couldn't quite work out what it was, but for the time being he concentrated on what he had. He had two footprints, which meant he had the man's natural stride.

He quickly looked around for the longest, straightest piece of wood he could find. He cut a branch off a bush with the machete and lopped off the leaves and twigs. That left him with a stick about a metre long. He placed the end by the heel of the first footprint and laid the wood down on the ground. Where it reached the heel of the second footprint he cut a small notch in the stick. He put the base of the tracking stick in the heel of the second print and swept it in an arc across the ground in front of him. The notch marked the distance at which the next footprint ought to appear – and there it was.

'Neat,' Brihony said when she saw what he was doing. He worked his way along the ground, step by step. Sometimes there were no prints, but thanks to the stick Beck knew where they should have been. Gradually, he was seeing the other clues more clearly too . . . Pebbles that were dislodged or over-turned – you could tell because the half that had been in the earth was darker from moisture. Bushes the man had brushed against – leaves generally grew in a set pattern, but some were twisted unnatu-rally in one direction. And always, every few metres, another footprint or two showed he was on the right track.

'Keep this up and we'll have him before sundown,' Brihony commented.

'Yeah, maybe . . .' Something was still niggling away at the back of Beck's mind. He couldn't pinpoint what it was, but for the time being he was doing all he could.

Until the trail vanished altogether. It led to the base of a boab, and stopped. The toes of the last footprint were right up against it, as if the man had stood with his face pressed to the bark. Or walked right into the tree.

They stood and stared at it. Brihony craned her neck back to peer up at the bare branches. There was nowhere up there that a man could hide.

Beck squatted down and studied the print closely. What was it that was bothering him? It was a normal footprint. It wasn't faked. The heel had dug into the ground, and the toes . . .

He groaned and clutched at his head, and slowly toppled over to one side. 'Aargh!'

'Beck?' Brihony knelt down, worried. 'What is it? What's wrong?'

'I'm totally out of practice! That's what's wrong! *Gaah!*' He climbed slowly to his feet, frowning with

154

annoyance. 'He led me right up the garden path. Right up it!'

'How do you mean?'

'Look. Watch my feet.' Beck took a few slow, deliberate steps. 'One, and two, and one, and two . . . heel first, then toes, right? The heel takes all my weight before the rest of my foot goes down. So the heel is always deeper than the toes.'

'OK . . .'

Beck squatted down again, and pointed at the footprints. 'Not here. The toes are deeper than the heels. He was walking *backwards*! This is where he started from, and he finished at the first footprint we found. It was another test. I should have known it was just too easy.'

Brihony groaned. 'You're kidding! Oh, that's *evil*! So what do we do now?'

Beck straightened up, and sighed. 'We backtrack, and we start again. But at least there's one thing.'

'What's that?'

'I recognize the sense of humour: no random guy would be trying to trick us like this. It's definitely Pindari!'

Chapter 19

This time, Beck paid more attention. He started at the single footprint and worked out the distance of a man's step. That gave him a starting circle. Pindari's other foot must have touched the ground somewhere inside it.

Imagining Pindari's foot pointing to twelve o'clock, then Beck found the answer at eight o'clock, where some grains of dirt looked out of place on the bare rock. They were clustered together in lumps but were too heavy for the wind to have blown them. They were stuck together because they had been damp when they got there. They had been transferred on the sole of a human foot. Beck had his first trace.

He used his tracking stick to mark out the line of

where the next footprint should be. There wasn't one, but there was a bunch of scrub grass that had been brushed to point in another direction. It didn't matter if Pindari had been walking forwards or backwards – the grass was pointing the way he had gone.

Bit by bit, trace by trace, Beck and Brihony worked their way along the trail. At first it was much slower than it had been when they were just following footprints, but Beck soon found himself settling into a rhythm. This time he tried not to walk with his eyes fixed on the ground right in front of him. It was more helpful to look five or ten metres ahead. It meant that you saw the traces coming, and it gave you a better idea of the landscape. Now and again he scanned ahead, just in case Pindari had come into view. He didn't want to be concentrating on the ground in front of his nose so hard that he ran slap into a patiently waiting Pindari.

The land was dry, the air wavering as far as he could see – the endless vista of rock and bushes and far-off sandstone cliffs. But if there had been someone out there, he would at least have seen a black dot moving through the shimmering air.

All he could see was a dark line on the horizon. Beck looked at it through narrowed eyes, then dismissed it. It looked a little like far-off rain clouds, but this was the dry season; it was probably just darker ground, the image distorted. He turned his attention back to the ground and set off again. He had to concentrate on the task in hand – tracking Pindari.

With his brain tuned to looking for traces, Beck found that they began to stand out from their surroundings again. Maybe a rock that had been overturned – the dark, damp sides fading as it dried out, but the dent in the ground still visible, showing where it had lain. Grass might be bent and broken, twigs scuffed in the direction of travel.

Sometimes the trail was obvious. Sometimes Beck still needed the tracking stick to show him where signs might be. Footprints came and went. It wasn't that Pindari was trying to hide his trail; it just depended on the hardness of the ground. His pace never changed much. If the toe prints had got deeper, and the heel prints all but vanished, that would have meant he was running. But he had kept going at the same steady plod – not too fast, not too slow, just the right speed to get where he was going without overheating. It was the best way to make progress through landscapes like this. It was the Aboriginal way.

That wasn't to say Pindari made it easy to follow him. There were still times when the trail seemed to vanish. He changed direction frequently, sometimes every few paces. Beck was still leaving marks for Barega and Ganan to follow, and he wondered what the men would make of these abrupt changes.

Pindari would zigzag over a stretch of clear ground, then cross bare patches of rock, where the footprints dried up completely and they had to search for other signs. At one point he had walked over a small rocky plateau about fifty metres wide. Brihony and Beck had to go round the edge to see where the trail picked up again, rather than trying vainly to work out his exact course. Once, the trail led into a dry, sandy area littered with rocks, and then vanished. Either Pindari had learned to fly, or he had simply jumped from rock to rock in a random fashion. They had to study the top of each one in turn for signs of dirt or scuff marks; then, when they found something, they had to check every rock within jumping distance and start again.

Sometimes Pindari did what any sane man in the middle of the Kimberley would do: he sought shade. If trees grew close together and cast a good shadow, he would stay beneath them for a while. It was easy to fall into the rhythm of the Outback. Time seemed to pass differently out here, with no distractions – no traffic, no music to listen to, no TV to watch. There was little to show time passing. When Beck looked at his watch at one point, he was only a little surprised to find that several hours had passed.

They would rest, they would take a sip of water, and then they would move on. If they passed a plant with berries or fruit that Beck could positively identify as edible, they would eat some. It kept their stomachs quiet without weighing them down, and it reduced the amount of water they needed to drink.

Water. Beck was uncomfortably aware that the bottle was growing lighter and lighter with every sip. On the boat, he had told the men they needed one and a half litres per hour when they were moving in the heat. He knew he and Brihony were already falling behind that target. They had set off from the bluff with maybe three litres in the bottle. If they were each going to drink one and a half litres per hour, that meant a maximum of two hours travel. They had done more than that already.

They needed more liquid. And there was only one source that Beck could think of.

'Uh, Brihony . . .' Beck swallowed and felt his face start to flush red.

She paused, and looked at him suspiciously. 'What?'

'You still got that seed pod I gave you?'

'Sure . . .' She pulled it out of her pocket, frowning. 'Why?'

'Because . . .' *Oh good grief*, he thought. He had been through all this with Pindari before, and it had been weird, but not embarrassing. But he and Pindari were male, and Brihony wasn't. That was what made it awkward. 'Look, if I was on my own I'd just use the water bottle, but we've got to share it, so . . . Look, I'll do it myself because I brought a pod along too, but . . .'

Brihony stared at him. She came and looked

him right in the eye, and held up the seed pod. 'Beck Granger, do you want me to *pee* into this and *drink it*?'

He nodded awkwardly.

'*Why?*'

'Because we're running low on water and we can't afford to waste anything. Straight out of the human body, urine is almost sterile. As long as your pee is clear, it's fine to drink and it'll help to hydrate you.'

'It might be fine to you.' She held his eye, then turned away in disgust. 'This thing we're after from Pindari? It had *so* better be worth it.'

They retreated in different directions. After a few moments they came back again.

Brihony's face was twisted in disgust. 'I cannot believe I just did that.' She glanced at Beck sideways. 'You did it too?'

He nodded. The taste had been . . . hard to describe. No one would be marketing a soft drink that flavour. But it had kept the fluids in his body, and that was what counted.

'Guess we won't be wasting water by washing our

hands,' she muttered. It was enough of a joke that they both couldn't suppress a small grin.

After another hour or so they came to another dry river bed. They stood at the top of a gentle slope. Beck looked from left to right and smiled at what he saw. At least one problem had just been solved.

Pindari had obviously climbed down – Beck could see the pebbles dislodged by his feet: they had slithered down after him. It looked like no water had fallen here for a million years. Bushes and trees had begun to reclaim the river bed for themselves.

The first priority was to see which way Pindari had gone, and it didn't take long. At the bottom of the bank, his feet had dug into the dry earth, picking some up and transferring it to the rocks. Instead of crossing to the other side, he had kept straight on down.

A hundred metres further along, they came to a point where the river bent round to the left. Beck beamed at Brihony. 'Fancy a proper drink?'

Her smile was weary. An afternoon of almost

nonstop walking in the heat of the Kimberley had taken its toll, though Beck knew she would never complain out loud.

'Something bubbly with ice would be great, thanks.'

'I'll see what I can do . . .'

He began to dig, scraping away at the top soil, with the machete still sheathed to protect the blade. The top layers were baked hard, but then they grew softer and damper. After a moment Brihony found a stick to help dig. Together they widened and deepened the hole. The soil that brushed against their fingers was pleasantly cool and moist.

Eventually it was more than just moist. Beck's fingertips were wet now. Water was slowly seeping into the hole they had dug. There was a little pool about a centimetre deep, but it was slowly filling up.

'We're on the outside of a bend in the river,' he said. 'When the water passes along, this is where it flows slowest and has the most time to sink into the ground.'

Brihony glared at him. 'You mean to say there's

enough water here to drink? That we drank that pee for nothing?'

Beck held up his hands apologetically. 'Not for nothing,' he said. 'In a survival situation, it's always a good idea to recycle your urine when you can. But hopefully this means we won't need to do it again!'

By now the pool was deep enough for him to hold the bottle under. Water bubbled and spluttered as it flowed in. When he picked it up again, it felt heavier. He had bought them a couple more hours of searching before he had to do this again.

'In an ideal world we would boil this before we drink it,' said Beck. 'But the soil's pretty sandy here, and that will have filtered out most of the impurities. I think we can chance it this once.'

Brihony smiled. 'Good work!'

They scooped water into their mouths with their hands. Before long the pool had filled up again so that Beck could top up the bottle a little more. Feeling stronger and invigorated, they set off after Pindari.

* * *

There weren't many bushes to brush against here, which meant that Pindari had left few signs. The bed itself was mostly smooth rounded stones or patches of dry earth. Pindari had tended to keep to the stones, so there were hardly any footprints.

Beck and Brihony gave up on the stones; instead, they split up and walked down either side of the river course, studying the banks. If Pindari had climbed out of the river bed, he would have gone up one bank or the other, and left prints. Eventually Beck found the traces on his side. Pindari had gone up at this point, so they followed him.

Beck wasn't surprised to find that he had chosen the far side of the river. If he had left it on the near side, he would have been doubling back on himself. Pindari's course was irregular, but he was always heading further and further into the Outback.

Beck checked his watch. It was late afternoon. He and Brihony would never make it back to their camp before dark, so they were committed to spending a night here in the Outback. There were a couple more hours of daylight left, though, so he decided to press on. Give it another hour, then construct a shelter for the night.

And then a rumble echoed across the Kimberley, and all Beck's plans changed.

It was a noise like the sky clearing its throat. It was so familiar that he took a moment to realize what it was. He stopped in his tracks and stared up at the sky ahead of them in horror. It was still blue and clear. Then he turned round and looked back the way they had come.

Behind, a wall of dark cloud stretched across his vision. The clear colours of the Outback blurred into a haze of rain.

'Beck Granger, you should have known that was coming!' Beck screamed in fury to the Outback in general.

He remembered that dark line he had seen earlier, on the horizon. He had put it out of his mind, because it was the dry season: he hadn't imagined that it might rain.

This was a freak rain storm, and they were the worst, because they struck without warning. They were violent and deadly.

167

'It's going to rain!' he shouted.

Brihony shrugged. 'Oh, great. We're going to get wet.'

Beck shook his head. 'We're going to drown if we don't do something.'

When it rained on ground that had been baked hot and hard for months, Beck knew it was like pouring water onto concrete. There was no way it could all soak in. Instead it just ran off. In an area like this a flash flood could grow out of nothing. Flash floods killed dozens of people each year – people caught out in the open, with nowhere to go. Beck hadn't exaggerated. They could easily drown.

Chapter 20

'OK,' Beck stated, 'we need a shelter, and we need it now.'

At least they weren't still in the river bed, he thought. A wall of water up to a metre high would soon come pouring down, washing everything away. Whatever happened to them up here, it wouldn't be as bad.

But it could still be grim if he didn't take care of things immediately.

A sandstone bluff rose out of the ground about twenty metres away. Beck immediately saw the possibilities for what he needed. Close by to it was a eucalyptus tree. About a metre from the ground, its trunk split into a Y. Higher up, the branches divided and divided again. The whole thing was crowned by a thick mass of green leaves that gave off a pungent, oily scent.

The rock face next to it overhung slightly, and there was a nook in it at about waist height. There would just be room for the two of them to crouch in there and shelter. The overhang would protect them from the rain.

But it wouldn't be very comfortable. They would be cold, and stuck there for however long the storm lasted. What Beck had in mind would be better than that.

He studied a clump of bushes the size of a garden shed. The stems and leaves were intertwined with long strands of ivy – which would be several metres long when pulled out straight.

'OK,' he said to Brihony. 'Get as much of this ivy together as you can. Try to keep it in one piece.'

She nodded and went to work, tugging all the long strands out of the bushes. Meanwhile Beck took the machete and climbed halfway up the tree. He spied out the branches that he wanted – the ones that were straightest, and long enough to reach from the tree to the rock face. It took several strong blows of the machete to sever each one. He felt the effort spreading like a warm glow inside him, and paused to take off his shirt. If he was hot and sweaty, then the shirt would grow damp, and in the evening, that would chill him rather than keeping him warm.

Eventually five or six branches of the right length lay at the foot of the tree. They all had smaller branches growing off them, each with a thick thatch of eucalyptus leaves. He clambered back down and started to hack the little branches off so that the main ones were bare poles.

Next Beck began to cut lengths off Brihony's growing pile of ivy and used this to tie the poles into a rectangular platform. He rested this on the lowest crook in the tree, and used more ivy to tie it firmly to the trunk. The other end rested on the shelf in the rock. The platform wasn't very wide, but it would be long enough for them to lie on.

The world flashed white. Beck looked up as a peal of thunder rolled across the Outback. He felt the ground vibrate, and his ears rang. As he watched, he saw another burst of lightning – a jagged dagger that flickered between Earth and sky, so bright that it left a green scar at the back of his eyes. Someone had once told him that in the north of Australia, ten people a year were killed by lightning. He didn't want to be the eleventh.

Part of the shelter was complete, but he needed more poles to make a roof for the platform. He had taken enough wood from the big eucalyptus, so he turned to a cluster of younger trees where the trunks were thinner, and started again.

Eventually Beck had five new poles. He tied the thickest two together at one end so that they made something like a large A without the crosspiece. He propped this against the rock so that the supports were on either side of the platform. Then he rested one end of a third pole in the notch where the two poles met, and the other on a higher branch of the eucalyptus so that it was above the platform. He tied the last two poles halfway up each support of the A at one end, securing the other end to the tree. It was like a framework above their bed platform.

Brihony had finished with her ivy pulling and had been watching for the last five minutes. 'Anything I can do?' she asked.

Beck thought. It would have been great if she'd had a machete too – this job would take half the time. But there was only one between them.

He nodded at the hollow in the rock. There was still half a metre of dry rock between the end of the platform and the back of the cleft. He took the fire steel from around his neck and passed it to her. 'Build a fire in there?'

'Sure thing.'

Brihony set to work while Beck started to put the finishing touches to the shelter. He had the bare bones – it just needed a roof. That would be made of the smaller eucalyptus branches he had cut off – a good pile now.

By now there was a cold wind warning of the approaching rain. A gust blew in his face. It ruffled his clothes and hair, carrying the smell of damp stone and dust.

On the side of the shelter nearest the rain, he began to lay leafy branches, propped up against the supports of the A-frame. He laid a complete row from tree to rock face, and tied them on with his dwindling supply of ivy. Then he added a second row, this one on top of the first layer. By the time he was done, that side of the shelter was a solid wall of eucalyptus, strong enough to shelter them from the wind and rain from that direction.

But the shelter still didn't have a totally covered roof, so on the downwind side he used the last of the eucalyptus to make as much of a covering as he could. The bottom half of that side was open to the elements, but there was no wind from that direction, and they shouldn't get too much draught.

Brihony had lit the fire. She had placed larger branches over the small pile of kapok fibre and kindling, and it was crackling away in its little nook. The wind was blowing it into a good flaming fire. Now she helped pass him branches and lengths of ivy, which made the work go faster. Beck laid the remaining eucalyptus leaves down on the platform as bedding. They would make it a little more comfortable to lie on.

And then it started to rain. The drops of water were hot and heavy on Beck's face. They fell onto the ground and stayed there, clinging to the dirt like silvery blobs for a few seconds, before very slowly sinking in.

'Just in time!' he said with a grin. He indicated that Brihony should climb into the shelter ahead of him. There was just room beneath the roof on the open side to squeeze through onto the platform. Beck pulled his shirt back on, and was immediately grateful for the little extra warmth that it gave, keeping the cold wind off. He reached up and pulled the boxers off his head. It felt a bit like getting home and kicking your shoes off. It meant he had arrived. This was where they were going to stay the night.

They sat side by side and looked out at a world that was suddenly very, very wet. The rain fell more heavily – and then it was as if someone had unzipped the sky and all the water in existence plummeted down to earth.

Beck glanced anxiously up at the makeshift thatch. If there were any weak spots, now was the time he would find out. If water could find a way through something, then it always took it. There were drops here and there, but nothing they couldn't avoid by shifting along a little.

Beads of rain gathered on the bottom edge of the roof. Within seconds they had turned into miniature streams of water. Beck held the bottle under one until it overflowed, and screwed the top back on.

'Beck . . .' Brihony said.

'Uh-huh?'

'A couple of hours ago, you made me drink my own pee.' Beck felt his face go red as she went on, 'I just want to say thanks. It was *so* worth it.'

'Uh . . . yeah.' Beck forced an embarrassed smile. 'Sorry about that. I drank mine too.'

'That's the only reason I'm still talking to you.'

They continued to look out. Their ears were battered by another blast of thunder, right overhead. In the distance, more daggers of lightning struck down at the world – one, two, three at a time.

'I also can't believe we're sitting in a tree, in a lightning storm,' Brihony pointed out.

Beck grinned. *Don't stand under a tree when there's lightning about* was always good advice.

'Lightning aims for the highest points, and there's trees higher than this one close by. If it hits anything, it will be them. We're safe-ish!'

He leaned forward to peer down at the ground.

They were a metre above what had been bone-dry soil. Now, water flowed by beneath them. Beck guessed it was knee deep. He couldn't quite see how fast it was running, so he plucked a leaf from the roof and dropped it. It hit the water and was swept away in the blink of an eye.

He watched it flow past the tree. All his work would have been for nothing if that eucalyptus was taken by the flood. But no – it was well rooted in the soil. It had probably stood up to hundreds of floods like this in its lifetime. *Just let it pass*, the tree was saying. *It will go, the waters will recede, and we can all get on with our lives again.*

'Safe – I hope,' he repeated quietly to himself.

The rain didn't last long, though the flood did, so they had no choice but to stay put. They emptied their pockets of the last quandongs and pieces of cooked snake. Brihony was nearest to the fire, so she could reheat the meat over the flames on a stick and pass it back to Beck.

Then they had the astonishing privilege of being able to watch a Kimberley sunset. The rain had washed the air clean, and the sky was a glowing mass of blues and reds and purples.

'I have eaten grubs and I've drunk wee,' Brihony murmured. There was awe in her voice as she looked out at the fluorescent layers of colour in the distance. 'And this almost makes it worthwhile.'

Beck knew what she meant.

But he also knew that they had been lucky. He should have been on the lookout for a storm like that. Was he getting careless as he grew up?

He resolved that it would not happen again. Tomorrow they would resume their search and he would be one hundred per cent focused on survival.

There was one thing he carefully didn't think about, because there was nothing he could do about it. He looked gloomily out at the rain. Every drop that fell would be wiping out the traces Pindari had left behind. All their searching today would have been for nothing, because tomorrow he would have nothing to follow.

Chapter 21

They slept uncomfortably, almost touching on their narrow platform. The leaves only made it slightly more comfortable. It was the kind of night where you weren't really sure if you'd slept or not.

Awake the moment the sun poked above the horizon, Beck wasn't surprised to see that the world on which it shone was now completely dry. The flood had gone. When he got down and felt the ground, it wasn't even damp.

He stretched and flexed his back and legs. Then he walked up a small rise, to gaze out over the Outback. The rain had washed the ground clean of dust, and the greens and reds and browns had never been brighter. Yet all Beck felt when he looked out at it was gloom at the thought of their lost trail.

'Why the long face?' Brihony asked when he came back to the shelter.

He braced himself, and then told her. 'The rain will have wiped out the trail. There's no way we can find Pindari now.'

Her face froze, and then she blinked and quickly looked away. Was it disappointment that they couldn't find Pindari and help the Jungun people? Beck wondered. Or anger that they wouldn't be able to get the people who'd hurt her mother? Or was she just unhappy at the thought of having to walk all the way back again?

'That's bad,' she replied.

'Plus, all the marks we made for the guys – they'll have gone too. Hopefully they'll have the sense to stay put, and we can make our way back. But don't worry, we'll keep on trying to find Pindari. It just won't be as soon as we'd have liked.'

'Well . . .' Brihony was trying to put a brave face on it. 'We should keep our strength up. What's for breakfast?'

He gave her a smile. 'Coming right up. I saw some boabs over there.'

The boab tree grew a short distance away. It towered high above them, its trunk bulging as if the wood inside was trying to get out. And this one had fruit dangling above his head, looking like leather water bottles: oval and long – almost the length of his forearm and hand together.

Ridges ran round and round the outside of the trunk, which made handy footholds for Beck to climb up. At the top, the branches forked: an empty stem dangled close by, but the nearest fruit was just out of reach of his fingers. He had to shimmy further along the branch, then pulled off two boab fruits and threw them down to Brihony.

Back at the shelter, he cut them open with the machete. The inside of the fruit was crammed with seeds embedded in a creamy white pulp. The taste was delicate, a little like chestnuts, and they both tucked in gratefully. With food inside him again, Beck felt stronger, his mind clearer.

'I wonder if Pindari ate from this tree?' Brihony said, through a mouthful of pulp.

'He could have . . .'

Then Beck put his piece of fruit down, and

stared thoughtfully back at the tree.

Yes, Pindari could have. It was the only boab tree in the area, and the wily Aboriginal man wouldn't let a source of food go untouched – would he?

And then Beck groaned and slapped his head. Brihony looked at him in alarm. He hurried back to the tree, and quickly scampered up it again – and there it was. Earlier, he had noticed the bare stem where a fruit had been. He could see where he had cut off the fruit higher up the branch. Here, the bare wood hadn't had time to dry and still glistened with sap. The first stump was darker and drier.

So where was the fruit that had been attached to it?

Pindari *had* eaten here.

Brihony had reached the base of the tree and was gazing up at him.

'The rain won't have washed away all the traces!' he called joyfully. He quickly climbed back down again. 'He had to eat, didn't he? He still left a trail!'

'Yeah, OK, but how do we know which way he was going?' Brihony asked practically. 'You've got to start in some direction.'

182

'Well, we know that he was heading north-east last night, so—'

And then another thing hit him. He couldn't believe it. *Two* obvious facts had been staring him in the face.

'When we first saw him, he was north-east of us. And last time we had his trail, he was still heading north-east. He's *always* been heading north-east. He's been zigzagging all over the place, turning left, turning right . . . but it all kind of averages out.'

'So . . .' Brihony said. 'If we keep on going north-east, and we have a close look at every tree or bush we find with the right kind of fruit and berries, we could still catch him.'

'Yup!' Beck was almost dancing with excitement, ready to be off.

'And I thought the footprints was hard. This could take for ever . . .'

'But at least we'll be doing something! Look, we'll just give it till this evening, right? One more day – and if we haven't found him by then, we turn back.' Suddenly it occurred to Beck that maybe Brihony had had enough of the Outback. 'That is, if you don't

183

mind another day of walking in boiling temperatures and eating more grubs, and, uh . . .'

She laughed. 'Yes, Beck, if it helps the Jungun, and helps get the guys who attacked my mother, I'll even drink my own wee again. So, put your pants back on your head! Let's hit the road!'

It was risky setting off into the Outback again with just a direction to follow, even though Beck knew he could keep them both alive – though not indefinitely. They had a full bottle of water, which wouldn't last, and no food. They needed a very good reason to keep heading away from civilization – but Beck was pretty certain they had one. They *could* still find Pindari. And for the sake of the Jungun, and Brihony's mum, and his own parents, they had to.

They moved slower than the day before. Beck wanted to look at every plant Pindari might have eaten from, and there were a lot of them. Bit by bit, he began to pick up the new trail. The bush with a stump where there had once been a cluster of berries. The empty husk of a boab fruit. Of course, there was always the risk that these had been eaten by animals, and there was probably plenty of stuff he was missing. But the new trail stuck to the roughly north-easterly direction, and Beck's heart leaped each time they found a new trace that looked human.

They ate as they went, the same way Pindari had – little and often. Beck no longer bothered leaving marks for Ganan and Barega to follow. The previous day's trail would have been washed away, and the men would not have risked coming after them. They would have stayed at the camp.

Although there was another possibility. As far as Beck remembered, the river curved northward. It was possible that he and Brihony were heading towards it again. He wondered if that would occur to the men – they could take the boat and come to meet them further on.

Either way, for the time being he would concentrate on tracking Pindari's eating trail without worrying about the others.

They came to a shallow, dried-out water hole and found the first sign that they were *definitely* heading in the right direction.

The hole was a circle of dry, cracked mud, too

deep for the rain to have washed away. There was still a little water left from the night before, though it was thick and scummy – if Beck had needed to drink from it, he would have dug a new hole like the previous day's.

A tree grew next to the hole, and someone had made a small hollow in the earth next to it, about thirty centimetres deep. It was too smooth and round to have been created by an animal. This was the work of human hands. Beck squatted and gazed at it as if it was the crown jewels.

'Pindari dug that?' Brihony asked.

'Someone did.' Beck cocked his head back to study the tree. He recognized it as a river red gum. He could just get his arms around the trunk, and it rose to the height of his head before twisting at a sharp angle. Thinner branches grew out of this top half, sprouting grey-green leaves. 'And I bet I know what he was after too.'

Beck began to excavate the sides of the hole with the machete, once again keeping it in its sheath to protect the blade. Something was moving in the crumbled pile of dirt. He gave it a poke with the machete, just in case it wasn't what he was after, but something with teeth or claws or venom. A maggot the size of a fat finger rolled into view. Its body looked like it was made of ten or twelve thick rings stuck together.

'Oh, boy,' Brihony exclaimed. 'Witchetty grubs!'

Beck grinned at the sight. These grubs were probably the most nutritious thing you could eat in the Outback. He had heard that a grown man could live off ten or so a day. He certainly had, before now. They weren't to unpleasant to eat either – a lot nicer than they looked. They lived on wood, which gave them a particular nutty flavour. This one would have been dining on the roots of the river red gum, so he was doing the tree a favour by removing it.

They kept digging and unearthed three more.

'So, are we just going to keep these for later too?' Brihony asked. 'I just don't fancy the thought of them wriggling around in my pockets.'

Beck grinned again. 'We can eat them now.'

He held a grub up to his mouth, paused a moment, then popped it in and bit down. It was too big to go in all at once. His teeth sliced down between the hard rings of its body. The contents exploded into his mouth like a mass of old, musty peanut butter. Aboriginals preferred the grubs cooked, when they tasted a bit like fried egg, but this was better than nothing. He chewed and swallowed, and then ate the other half with a grimace.

Brihony's jaws were soon working away at her own grub, and the look of distaste on her face was gradually fading. 'OK . . . That's still pretty disgusting.'

Beck smiled and handed her a second grub. She took it reluctantly. She knew they needed all the energy they could find.

There was a down side to finding the witchetty grubs, Beck thought as they continued their way. They were big. If Pindari had eaten a few, he would be feeling comfortably full. He might not pick any more berries as he went. The signs might disappear now.

Sure enough, the trail seemed to vanish again. Beck went from bush to bush and tree to tree, and widened his search to fifty metres or more from the direction in which they were headed. No luck. He squared his shoulders and gritted his teeth, and kept going north-east.

Brihony was forcing herself to be cheerful. 'Go far enough north-east,' she said, 'and we'll be back in Darwin. Or else we'll miss it and fall into the sea.'

'We just have to keep looking,' Beck said quietly. Then he remembered that he had promised they would call a halt if they hadn't found Pindari by the evening. That is, if the man they were following really *was* Pindari. Maybe he had been wrong about the first footprint. Maybe it hadn't been a test. Maybe Beck wasn't as clever as he thought he was. Maybe it was some Aboriginal guy going walkabout who didn't want a couple of whitefella kids sticking their noses into his business – or thought it would be hilarious to lead them on a wild-goose chase.

At noon they sheltered in the shade of some trees. It took a couple of hours for temperatures to drop a little. Beck seethed with impatience, which he knew was a very bad idea in the Outback. Nothing here could be forced or hurried if you wanted to stay alive. He made himself wait, and two hours after the sun had passed overhead, off they went again.

They followed Pindari's trail – or what Beck hoped was Pindari's trail – as the afternoon moved on and began to turn into evening. Beck kept an eye out for more dark clouds gathering on the horizon, but none showed. They continued to eat as they went. The level of the water in the bottle fell, so they dug down in another river bed and drank. Their pee was now too dark to help keep them hydrated. That also worried Beck. He knew they were facing a ticking time-bomb of dehydration.

He knew he should call a halt soon. Stop. Drink the water bit by bit to replenish their levels. Stay overnight, and then – though it broke his heart – admit defeat and head back to join the others. They wouldn't be following a trail so there would be nothing to slow them down. They could just head back south-west. The sun was low on the horizon now. By this time the next day they could be back at the river with Barega and Ganan.

'Beck!' Brihony grasped his arm and pointed. 'Look! Is that smoke?'

Beck stopped and stared into the distance. She was right. A thin column of smoke drifted up from some high ground dead ahead. It looked like a straight pencil line drawn over the blue sky. And it was like an arrow pointing for them, saying, *Your destination is here*.

Chapter 22

All thoughts of giving up disappeared, but before they went on, Beck took care to fill up the bottle from the hole.

'My dad used to say that when you most want to quit, it means you are probably closest to your goal,' he said.

He smiled, but didn't look up until the bubbles had stopped and the bottle was full. 'And I *knew* we were almost there.'

'We don't *know* it's Pindari. Just because we've been searching all day and we really want it to be him doesn't mean we've found him, Beck. It could be some hiker. It could be some fool who dropped an empty bottle which acted as a magnifying glass for the sun's rays, and now a wildfire is about to sweep through the Outback. Assume nothing.' Brihony was playing with Beck's mind.

Beck smiled, then stood up to take a direction check. It was fast approaching twilight. Another hour and it would be dark; then the smoke column would be invisible. They had to get to it before it disappeared.

'North-east,' he said with purpose. 'OK, let's finish this. Coming?'

Even though Beck was trying hard not to feel too excited, just in case they were disappointed, he couldn't deny the extra spring in his step, as if he were embarking on the final lap of a race – the bit where new energy flows into you even though you're sure you've given everything.

They crossed another dry stream, and then it was a twenty-minute slog up a slight rise. It started out as a gentle gradient, but by the time they finished they were on hands and knees. They crested the ridge and saw . . . nothing. Just more Outback stretching away into the dusk. But now Beck could smell wood smoke, and there was a glimmer of orange light ahead. They continued until they came to the edge of a hollow.

Their eyes went to the fire first, because it was the brightest thing – orange and crackling with light and energy. A spit had been set up across it: two small A-frames on either side, with a stick joining the tops across the flames. Something that Beck was pretty sure was a wallaby leg was slowly roasting on it.

The old man beside the fire sat so still they didn't notice him at first. He squatted with his knees up around his ears. He was powerfully built, with wide shoulders and a broad chest. He wore ragged cut-off jeans and a grimy top. His hair and beard were a mass of white curls against his dark skin. A spear was thrust into the ground next to him.

His stillness was infectious. Beck felt as if his own feet were taking root in sympathy. He made himself put one foot in front of the other, and walked into the circle of firelight.

The man spoke. He had an Australian accent that overlaid something deeper and older. Beck had heard Aboriginal people speaking their own language. It was singsong and very rapid so that the sounds ran together. This man seemed to be forcing himself to slow down so that Beck would be able to understand.

'I thought it was you, but you've grown so. From where I was standing I couldn't be sure.'

Beck's heart pounded with joy. It *was* Pindari. The man they had been looking for; the man who had taught him everything that had got them this far. He wanted to shout with joy and pump the air and go '*Yes!*' but that was not Pindari's way.

And so he made himself answer in the same calm, level tone: 'So you set me a little test, Uncle?'

Pindari was not his uncle, of course, or any kind of relation. Among Pindari's people, younger people used 'Uncle' and 'Aunt' to address older people whom they respected. It was also an honour for the younger people to be allowed to use these names. When Beck had met Pindari, he addressed the old man only as 'Elder'. The first time Pindari had invited him to call him 'Uncle', Beck had felt like he had received some special honour.

'Only one of my mob – or someone I had taught – would have managed it,' Pindari said. 'After the rain, I suppose you followed my eating trail?'

'Well, obviously, Uncle. It was the first thing that occurred to me.'

For the first time Pindari looked up at them, and Beck saw the glimmer of humour in his dark eyes.

'Obviously,' the old man agreed, and Beck realized that Pindari knew he had been on the verge of giving up.

'Hang on!' Brihony interrupted. 'Oh – by the way, I'm Brihony. But what do you mean, you couldn't be sure from where you were standing? When we saw you, you were so far away you couldn't have seen anything!'

Pindari fixed her with a dark gaze. 'That was when *you* saw *me*.'

Ha! So *he* had seen *them* long before. Beck pondered, *I wonder how close the old man got*.

'You must be Mia Stewart's girl.' Pindari waved a hand. 'Sit down, both of you. Got a knife, Beck? Of course you have. Cut yourself some meat.'

The meat was dark red and tender. The machete easily sliced through it. It sizzled, and juices dripped off the blade. Beck felt his stomach rumbling as he passed Brihony a slice, then cut one for himself. Without knife or fork or plate there was no polite way

196

to eat it, so they had to cup their free hands under their chins to catch the drops.

'You must tell me how you come to be wandering about in the Outback, but first' – Pindari raised his voice slightly – 'if those two jokers behind me don't show themselves, I'll spit them like I spitted this wallaby.'

Huh? Beck and Brihony both jerked their heads up and stared into the darkness behind Pindari. They hadn't heard anything.

After a pause, a familiar voice spoke:

'No need for that, Uncle.'

Part of the darkness moved, and two figures emerged into the firelight. Brihony and Beck's mouths dropped open in surprise.

'It's you! How did you get here?' Brihony asked.

'Brihony, Beck – hi.' Barega stood there with his hands on his hips and a big grin on his face. 'We got the boat fixed and came up the river. It makes a big loop – we're only about quarter of a mile from it here. We saw the fire; came to investigate.'

Ganan came to stand beside him. A rucksack dangled from his hand. 'Greetings, Uncle Pindari.'

He nodded to the older man. 'May we share your fire?'

Pindari scowled up at them. 'You know me. I don't know you.'

Barega's smile faded a little under the old man's hostility. 'It has only been a year or two, Uncle. You saw us more recently than you saw Beck.'

'I have reason to remember Beck.' Pindari's voice was cold. 'He is a friend to the Jungun. A follower of the old ways. Not a man who runs off to the white-fella's world at the first opportunity. Why should I remember one like that?'

Beck and Brihony exchanged anxious glances. The last thing they wanted was for the three to fall out. They were all meant to be in this together.

'They are our friends, um, Uncle,' Brihony said. Pindari's eyebrow went up when she used that word, but he didn't object.

'They have important news for the Jungun,' Beck added. 'That's why we're all here.'

Pindari thought for a moment more. 'I remember you,' he said to the two men. He made it sound like he had made a decision to remember, rather than

just dragging their names out of his memory. 'Ganan
. . . Barega – sit down. Beck, tell me why we're all
here.'

'It's important news, Uncle . . .' Ganan began.
Pindari's gaze stayed fixed on Beck, and it was clear
he wasn't listening to anyone else. Ganan trailed
away into silence and gave Beck the go-ahead with
his eyes.

'We've come to finish what my parents started,'
Beck said. 'Lumos wants to buy the Jungun land. We
think they will do to it what they did to the Yawuru.
We want to stop them.'

'Lumos,' Pindari mused. 'What they did to the
Yawuru was an evil thing. No, they must not be
allowed to take any more land. We are now right on
the edge of the Yawuru land that was polluted. That's
why I stopped here – I didn't want you going into it. *I*
don't like going into it. It is a bad place.' He
shuddered. 'Poisons in the food and water. The land
hurts.'

'Beck's parents gave you something, Uncle,
before they died,' said Ganan.

Pindari held his thumb and forefinger apart. 'They

gave me a small plastic whitefella thing. About that big. They said it was very important, though it was useless to me.'

Ganan took a deep breath, poised to explain the concept of USB sticks, but Pindari carried on: 'I mean, I don't have electronic computers out here, so what was I going to do with it?'

Beck grinned as Ganan let the breath out again. The other man looked annoyed at being led up the garden path.

'We're hoping you kept it, Uncle,' said Barega.

'Of course I kept it. It's in a cave, guarded by the ancestors.' Pindari made a chopping motion with his hand into the darkness. 'That way, on the edge of Jungun land.'

'Hold on, Uncle.' Ganan delved into his bag and pulled out a map, which he unfolded on the ground between him and Pindari. 'Can you show us? We're here . . .'

He pressed a finger to the paper, and Beck peered down at it. The river curved in a loop that was so long it was almost a circle. There was a narrow neck of land a few miles across where the river didn't quite join up. They were very close to it.

He was puzzled to see some rectangles that looked very out of place in the middle of the Outback. But then he remembered: Lumos's pollution had come from a uranium mine. Those squares must be the deserted buildings.

'Can you show us on this where the cave is?' Ganan asked.

Pindari shot him a look of pure contempt. 'I have no use for maps.'

'No, but *we* do . . .' Barega said hopefully.

'The land is the land. It belongs to itself. It will not be confined to a piece of paper. I will tell you where the cave is. It is at the bottom of a high cliff, very hard to reach. It is by the water's edge, but high enough up that it never floods.'

Ganan looked thoughtfully into the darkness, in the direction that Pindari had indicated, then down at the map again. 'That must be the very edge of the land that Lumos wants,' he said.

'Then it is right that the stick is kept there. The ancestors will watch over it in the sacred cave.'

'Actually,' Ganan said, 'I was just thinking that it's

kind of ironic.' He fumbled again in his bag as he spoke. His tone was sneering.

Pindari gave him a hard stare, then deliberately turned his attention to Beck. It was clear that he was cutting the other man out of the conversation. 'The ancestors will guide you. Follow the spears—'

The harsh crack of a gunshot suddenly echoed through the night. Pindari's face, so full of life and expression, grew slack and cold. The old man toppled to the ground while the front of his shirt turned slowly red.

Chapter 23

Beck scrambled to his feet and ran across to Pindari. But he lay completely still, his eyes open and staring. Pindari was gone. Beck's heart turned over with anger and horror, but he forced himself to think straight. He stared out into the darkness all around.

His eyes darted around the campsite, trying to work out where the shot had come from. They were completely at the mercy of whoever had fired out of the darkness. But Beck couldn't see anyone. Then he turned slowly as it dawned on him that the killer was right here in the camp with them.

Ganan and Barega were on their feet, and Ganan held a gun – a sleek black automatic pistol that fitted snugly into his hand. Brihony and Beck both stared at him, their minds spinning, working overtime to try and make sense of what had happened. Brihony was sobbing, wide-eyed with shock.

Barega also looked shocked, but Beck realized it was nothing like the shock that he and Brihony felt. But the gun wasn't pointed at Barega. It was pointed at *them*.

'You didn't need to—' Barega began.

'Shut up.' The gun moved from Brihony to Beck, and back again.

'You?' Brihony gasped. 'You're working for Lumos?'

'Too right,' said Ganan.

'How much are they paying you?' Beck asked quietly. His heart pounded. He could already see where this was going. There was no alternative. Ganan had murdered an old man in front of him and Brihony. They were witnesses, and that meant they only had seconds to live unless he could think of something.

'Enough.'

'There wasn't meant to be any killing!' Barega's voice was shrill. 'We could have taken the stick and handed it over, and these guys would never have known anything!'

'Yeah, well . . .' Ganan half turned towards Barega and the gun moved with him. For a just a moment it wasn't pointing at anyone. Beck tensed himself to leap at it. 'It didn't work out like that!'

'Yeah, you could have just stabbed us in the back without ever telling,' Brihony shouted through her tears. The gun snapped back to point at her, and Beck held himself back. 'So who were those goons who attacked us in Broome?'

'Just a little nudge in the right direction.' Ganan tightened his grip on the gun.

'A *nudge*?' Brihony was becoming furious. Her fists clenched and she seemed to be preparing to launch herself at the man with the gun. 'You could have killed my mother, or left her brain-damaged – for a *nudge*?'

'We needed Beck, and it looked like he wasn't going to take the bait, despite all our efforts. The PlaceSpace mystery, the white dragon – even telling him about his parents. It was all supposed to draw him in. But despite all that, you were going to say no, weren't you, Beck? And we couldn't have that.'

Brihony's fury was infectious. Beck felt some of it start to creep into him. These men didn't care who they used, who got hurt, just as long as they got what they wanted: money. The memory of his parents was like a priceless jewel in his head. These guys had just treated it like trash – another pawn in their little game.

But Beck was calm enough to notice something. The gun barrel moved as Ganan spoke, from Beck to Brihony and back again. Beck wondered if he was deciding which one to shoot first, or just trying to summon the courage to pull the trigger. Ganan wasn't a born killer. He lacked practice.

And Beck had seen that he couldn't even keep them covered if he was distracted. *So, please*, he thought, *let him be distracted again. Let him move the gun away, just a little . . .*

Barega gave him the opportunity. 'Ganan, mate,' he pleaded, 'don't do this . . .'

Ganan drew a breath to answer, and once again turned away. Again the gun wasn't pointing at anyone.

Beck leaped forward. In one smooth motion he pulled the machete from its sheath and brought the back of it down hard on Ganan's wrist. He used the blunt edge of the blade – he only wanted to disarm Ganan, not cripple him. But it was still like hitting him with an iron bar. The man howled and dropped the gun as his wrist went numb. Beck hoped he had broken it.

He hadn't thought much further ahead than that. What would he do now? Maybe he should pick up the gun and throw it away into the darkness. But it had fallen at Barega's feet.

It was Brihony who solved that problem. Ganan was still dancing in a little circle of agony, clutching his wrist, his face screwed up in pain. Brihony scooped something up off the ground, ran forward and dropped it down the back of his neck.

'Let's see how you do with a funnel web!'

Funnel web – two words that made Beck's blood run cold. The funnel web spider was one of Australia's most poisonous. Its bite was agonizing.

Ganan shrieked. 'Get it off! Get it off!' He tugged at his T-shirt in panic, and Barega went to help him.

'Come on!' Brihony ran as fast as she could in the other direction. Beck hesitated – he still wanted that gun. *'Come on!'*

Beck realized they were out of time, so he turned and ran after her. He glanced back after they had gone a short distance. They were well out of the circle of firelight. Ganan had finally managed to pull his shirt off and was stamping on it.

'It could have bitten you,' Beck gasped.

Brihony poked him in the arm. 'It was just dirt. I only *said* it was a spider.'

And Beck had to grin. To Ganan, the earth running down his back would have felt very similar to a spider's legs.

But they couldn't stop to enjoy the sight. In just a few seconds the men would come looking for them. Running wouldn't solve anything. The men had longer legs, and sooner or later they would catch up. And Ganan still had that gun. So Beck knew that he and Brihony had to think smarter – and fast.

He reached out for her arm and slowed her down. She stared at him through the gloom as if he was mad. They could barely see each other. The sky was as brilliant with stars as ever, but the land was just vague grey shapes. The men would only see them if they were silhouetted against the Milky Way. Beck pulled her down into a crouch and they looked back at the camp.

Ganan and Barega were both circling the fire at the edge of the light, straining their eyes into the darkness. They had been too preoccupied with getting the spider out of Ganan's clothes to notice which way the two friends had run.

Then Ganan pulled a pair of torches out of his backpack. He tossed one to Barega, and two spears of light flicked out into the darkness.

Beck closed his fist around a small rock. When both men were looking the other way, he rose swiftly and drew his arm back. Taking care not to grunt with the effort, he flung the rock as hard as he could across the camp. It landed with a thud on the far side of the fire. Immediately Barega and Ganan swung their torches round in the direction of the sound. Beck heard them speaking, but not their words, as they ran off into the darkness.

'Come on,' he murmured. He and Brihony headed off in the other direction.

'We can't keep doing that,' Brihony murmured

back – they both knew that a voice could carry a long way in the still night air.

'We're not going to.'

He and Brihony found themselves at the edge of a gully, and they made their way carefully down the side. Beck didn't want to dislodge any stones that would rattle down the slope and alert their enemies. Nor did he want to trip over something in the dark and end up injured. They couldn't afford to use a light, even if they had one – so their only option was to find somewhere to hide down in the gully.

They made their way cautiously through the dark until Beck found what he wanted: a dense clump of bushes growing at the base of a large rock. He knelt down beside the rock and felt his way carefully with the machete. A small voice at the back of his mind screamed that he must be mad – hiding under a bush in the pitch black when anything could be lurking there! Maybe another king brown . . . But he didn't have a choice. If there *was* anything nasty, he hoped the machete would scare it off before it decided to investigate the annoying mammal on the other end.

He led the way into the bush and Brihony followed him. They lay there staring at each other from a distance of a few centimetres. Brihony's face was pale in the dark. Too pale, Beck decided. His would look the same – visible to anyone close by who was looking in their direction.

'Hang on . . .' he whispered. He spat on his fingertip and ground it into the dirt, then smeared damp mud in streaks on Brihony's face. He repeated the process on his own. 'Camouflage. Breaks up the lines. Our brains are programmed to pick out faces.'

They heard the men's voices coming and going. It must have been half an hour or more before they heard them clearly. Then they both froze as torchlight flashed down the gully and through the leaves. Shadows danced over them as the light moved. Neither of them shifted a muscle.

'Anything?' It was Ganan, a short distance away. His voice sounded harsh and abrupt.

'Nothing. Still nothing.' Barega was almost on top of them. His voice seemed to boom in Beck's ear. 'Face it, Ganan. They're miles away.'

Ganan swore. 'OK, that's it. We'll leave them

to the dingoes. They won't get out of here alive.'

'Pindari seemed to think Beck could make it.'

'Pindari was a stupid old man who believed his ancestors haunted a cave.' The contempt from Pindari's murderer made Beck's blood boil. 'I'm not interested in what he thought. C'mon – let's at least get back to the boat and sleep in a decent tent. We'll find the cave when it's light.'

The torch beam swept over their hiding place one last time as Barega turned slowly round. It made Beck think of a lighthouse. But then they heard his footsteps recede, and the clatter of falling rocks as he scrambled up the side of the gully.

The men were gone, but Beck wasn't moving. He and Brihony lay where they were for the rest of the night, until the world began to emerge from the pitch dark, and sunlight spilled again across the Outback.

They cautiously returned to the camp as the sun rose above the horizon. Their shadows were long in the fresh colours of a new day. Pindari lay where the men had left him. Beck knelt down by the body. He reached out to feel for the pulse in the old man's neck, but there was nothing. Pindari must have died instantly. Beck felt relieved that he had at least been spared the pain of betrayal by two of his fellow Jungun. And at the same time he felt sick to his core that someone he had loved and respected so much was gone.

'We'll get them.' Brihony spoke with quiet contempt. 'You can get us back to civilization, can't you? And we'll go public. We'll tell everyone . . .'

'Our word against theirs,' Beck said. 'I know Al will believe us and he'll do what he can, but Lumos will just deny they had anything to do with it. They'll simply make Ganan and Barega disappear.'

Brihony's face sagged in despair. 'So it's over? We just go home empty-handed and forget about it?'

'Nope.' Beck rose slowly to his feet and looked out at the horizon. 'We go home with the stick.'

'But how? The men—'

'The men are in the boat, which has to stick to the river – which loops, if you remember.' Beck closed his eyes and summoned up the details of the map in his mind. 'They're taking the long way. We can just cut across.'

'The land's poisoned.'

'I can keep us safe.' Beck spoke with quiet assurance.

'And then?' Brihony asked.

'We figure out a way back to civilization and make sure the right people see what's on that stick.'

'Can you really keep us alive?'

'I'll do my best,' he said with a smile.

Hope began to flicker on Brihony's face, but she still pointed out the difficulties. 'Pindari said that the cave is very hard to get to.'

'But not impossible. Do you think *he* had a boat? You must be able to reach it by land as well as by water.'

'We don't know where it is.'

'We know it's just above the edge of the river, over there . . .' Beck gestured in the direction Pindari had indicated the night before. Beck and Brihony had been sitting opposite him, and the old man had pointed just over Beck's shoulder.

'OK, so we've got a vague direction—'

'No.' Despite all that had happened, Beck couldn't help smiling. He felt the confidence swelling within him. 'Can you imagine Pindari being vague about anything? He knew the Outback like the back of his hand. If he pointed in a direction, he meant it exactly. So – I was sitting here; Pindari pointed . . .'

He slowly turned to face the direction they were heading for.

'The cave's that way.' He dug his heel into the dry ground to draw a line. 'Let's go get that stick.'

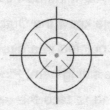

Chapter 24

It didn't take long to gather together what they needed. Pindari had a water bottle, so now they had one each. He had also been carrying a large leather bag that probably contained everything he owned. Beck cut up the wallaby into slices and stowed them inside the bag. There would be enough to last them a couple of days.

Lumos had poisoned the land they would be crossing, so they couldn't risk eating or drinking anything there. Everything had to be carried with them.

And then there was one last thing. Pindari himself.

Tears pricked behind Beck's eyes as he stood over the old man's body. It wasn't just that he had lost a friend. It wasn't just outrage and shock at witnessing a callous murder. He would have felt that with anyone's death. All life is special. But *so much* had been locked away inside Pindari's head. So much wisdom, so much knowledge, so much experience. It had just been wiped out. Beck knew that a truly great man had died – and with him was lost a library of knowledge.

Pindari still lay as he had fallen, eyes open, body half curled up. Beck didn't know enough about the funeral rites of the Aboriginal people. What should he do?

They didn't have a spade to dig a grave, and digging a hole with the machete or a stick in the hard, dry ground would take for ever. It would waste time, and wasting time would have annoyed Pindari.

Brihony came to stand beside Beck and put a hand on his shoulder. Her voice shook. 'There's nowhere else he would have wanted to die.'

Beck nodded silently. She had answered the question for him. Pindari had belonged to this land, and this land would reclaim him. The dingoes would come for his body if nothing else got there first.

But Pindari would never want to meet them curled up like that. So Beck knelt down and gently rolled him over onto his back, then straightened his legs, crossed his arms over his chest, and closed his eyes.

Brihony watched him. 'I've never seen a dead person before.'

'Pindari's spirit has long gone. This is just his earthly remains.'

Beck tugged Pindari's spear out of the ground and put it in the old man's hands. Now Pindari's body could face whatever came for him with pride.

Beck passed Brihony the water bottle they had shared ever since the boat accident, and took Pindari's for himself. Then he swung the leather bag onto his back and raised his watch to the sun for a northerly reading. He glanced down at the line he had drawn in the sand. On the face of his watch, the direction they wanted was five minute marks away from north.

'Come on,' he said, and set off without a backward glance.

They were walking into the loop of land that was almost encircled by the river. Whichever way they went, they would eventually reach water. Finding Pindari's cliff was more difficult. Every few minutes

Beck took another reading to check they were still going the right way.

They were now heading into the land that Lumos had poisoned. The mine buildings that Beck had seen on the map were still some miles away; they wouldn't pass anywhere near. But their influence was all around, and he and Brihony found the first sign of it when they came to a dry watercourse.

Every river and stream bed they had seen so far still managed to bring forth new life. Trees and bushes grew out of the pebbles, kept alive by the water that had soaked into the soil.

Not in this one. The withered remains of dead plants clung to the rocks, but that was all. There had been rainy seasons since the disaster. Enough fresh water had come down this way to wash most of the vegetation away. But the soil was still poisoned. Nothing new grew here, or ever would. This land, which could have produced so much new life, had been killed by Lumos, just as Pindari had been killed by Ganan. Everything that was special and unique . . . just wiped out. The sheer waste of it made anger boil up in Beck's heart.

He remembered the images on Ganan's iPad back in the warehouse in Broome. It all seemed so long ago, though it had only been three nights back. Ganan hadn't been lying about the effects of the contamination – which made his betrayal all the more wicked. He knew exactly what kind of people he was working for, and yet he still took their money.

Beck checked the direction again, and they headed across the dry course.

'Will the air be radioactive?' Brihony asked quietly.

He shook his head. 'Air blows away. It was water-containment pools that cracked, remember? The water in them would have been toxic. So anything that the water touched would be poisoned. And anything that ate anything – and so on. It would have soaked into the soil, been picked up by plants . . . but the air will be OK.'

'It could get through our boots,' she pointed out.

'We'll keep moving. It won't get the chance.'

As they continued across the doomed land, the scrub grew withered and brown. It crumbled when their trousered legs brushed against it. The boabs and the eucalyptuses that had provided shelter and fruit were just wooden skeletons. No leaves or fruit hung from their branches. The wood was dried out and brittle. Beck wanted to poke one with his machete, just to see how far in it would go. Then he changed his mind. For all he knew, he might push the whole thing over. It would be one more act of environmental vandalism and Beck wasn't like that.

Something else was bothering Beck. A cloud of unease hung over him. Was he sensing the land's hurt? It bothered him as they walked along in silence.

Then Brihony, walking up a short slope, dislodged some pebbles with her foot. They clattered down, and Beck jumped with shock. But now he realized what had been worrying him. The land was so *quiet*.

There had always been sounds in the Kimberley. The wind blowing through trees and shrubs. The cries of a dozen different types of bird. Insects buzzing as they flapped their wings or rubbed their legs together.

But here there was nothing. This part of the Outback was as quiet as the grave because it *was* a grave.

Beck set a punishing pace. He wanted to be out

of this zone of death as soon as possible, and he was aware that Ganan and Barega were heading for the same place as they were. The men might have taken the longer route, and they had probably set off later – but they had an engine.

They took rest stops, because it would have been suicidal not to. There would be no point reaching the cave first if they arrived dehydrated and weak from hunger. But their breaks only lasted a few minutes. They sat on a high rock that was clear of the poison from the pools. A sip of water, maybe a nibble of wallaby meat, and then they were off again. All they could do was take long, measured strides to eat up the ground in front of them, and hope that they would be in time.

Finally, halfway through the afternoon, the ground fell away in front of them and they gazed down at a river gorge. They stood on the edge of a sheer cliff of red sandstone that fell fifty metres, straight down to the water. Beck looked quickly up and down the gorge. There was no sign of a boat.

'We're first?' Brihony asked.

He allowed himself a small smile, but he wasn't going to get carried away now. 'I reckon we are . . .' He saw that Brihony was peering down the cliff, a frown on her face. 'Will you be OK?'

'I guess I'll have to be. Any chance of a bite to eat and a drink?'

'Sure. We may as well keep our strength up.'

Brihony walked up and down the edge of the cliff while Beck swung the bag off his back. 'This is definitely the place?'

'This is definitely where he was pointing,' Beck answered with quiet confidence. He had faith in his navigation and Pindari's accuracy.

'So where do we climb down?'

'Let's scout out a good place.'

Brihony continued to patrol the cliff top while she drank from her bottle. Suddenly, a few metres to Beck's left, she stopped. She was staring straight down at the ground. Then she crouched. 'Hey, Beck, look!'

'What is it? A sign saying *Climb down here*?' Beck hurried over.

'Good as. See?'

He knelt down beside her. It took him a moment to see it. When he did, he whistled.

A figure was carved into the rock, the grooves only about a centimetre deep. It was like the footprints he had tracked – if you looked straight at it, then it was hard to make out. You had to view it from an angle, so that there were areas of light and shade. It showed a man brandishing a spear very like the one Beck had left with Pindari's body.

Somehow you could tell that this figure belonged. The lines followed the curves of the rock, as if whoever had carved them had been careful to make it blend into the untamed nature of the Outback. It must have been thousands of years old.

The man's spear pointed straight towards the edge of the cliff.

'He said, follow the spears, remember?' Brihony pointed out.

'Then I guess that's what we do . . .'

Chapter 25

At first Beck couldn't see anything unusual in the place where the spear was pointing, and he was about to move on. But then he peered more closely over the edge of the cliff.

There was a ledge. It was the same reddish colour as the sandstone, and from this angle it was almost invisible. It angled gently downwards.

That was the good news. The bad news was that it wasn't much wider than the length of his feet.

'We can't walk down that!' Brihony was aghast when Beck pointed it out.

'Nope. We'll have to ease our way carefully. And we'll have to go down facing the rock. If we had our backs to the cliff, our bums would push us off. I'll go first,' he said.

'Word of advice, Beck?' Brihony said as he crouched down by the edge of the cliff and lowered himself onto the ledge, first one foot, then the other.

'Uh-huh?' He began to move sideways to make room for her.

'If you ever meet someone really special – you know, a girl you really fancy – and want to give her a good time . . .'

'Yeah?'

Brihony lowered herself to stand beside him. All her weight was on her arms until her feet touched the ledge. 'Don't do something like this. She won't like it.'

'Thanks. I'll bear that in mind . . .'

Slowly, inch by inch, arms and legs spread out, they made their way along the ledge. The cliff in front of their faces was cool and smooth. Because the ledge sloped, every new step was slightly lower than the last one. The first time Beck bent his legs, his knees pushed against the rock as if trying to over-balance him; instead, they had to twist their legs round as far as they could, spread-eagled against the stone. It was nerve-racking work and tiring on the

226

limbs; soon their legs felt as if they were being slowly twisted out of their sockets.

Try as Beck might, he couldn't turn his head enough to see how far down they had come. All he could do was keep going.

The end came abruptly when the ledge vanished into thin air: Beck's right foot came down where it had been expecting rock – and there was nothing.

'*Whoa!*'

He scrabbled at the rock with his fingers, and Brihony grabbed hold of his shirt. He managed to pull himself back so that both feet were on rock again, and peered down. There was no more ledge. On the plus side, they were only about five metres from the rocks at the bottom of the cliff.

'Bit more climbing, I'm afraid . . .' he told Brihony.

'Oh, I'm totally in the zone,' she said through clenched teeth.

They crouched gingerly, and began to climb down the final few metres side by side. There wouldn't have been room at the bottom between the cliff and the river for Beck to stand back and call out a route to her, as he'd done before. This was the only way to do it. Beck could have got down in half the time, but he made himself move at Brihony's pace.

In five more minutes they were at the foot of the cliff. They stood on a thin line of boulders that ran along the water's edge.

'Think there'll be crocs here?' Brihony asked.

'I doubt it. No other animal would be stupid enough to climb down that cliff, so they won't associate this place with food.'

'Hope you're right. OK – what next?'

'Dunno. Look for a cave? Or look for spears . . .'

They went in separate directions, and Brihony was the first to call out. Beck hurried back to find another carved man, his spear pointing straight up at the sky. He craned his head back. About three metres above them he saw a dimple in the cliff face. He couldn't tell if it was a cave or not. The top of it overhung, so it would be invisible from above.

'We've got to climb again . . .' Brihony moaned.

'Yeah, but not far. I'll go first to check it out.'

Beck covered the distance quickly while Brihony waited by the river. She hugged herself and, despite Beck's reassurances, kept a careful eye on the water for crocodiles. In a matter of moments Beck had reached the edge of the recess, and now he could see that it was a dark hole that led into the rock. He looked back down at Brihony with a huge smile on his face.

'Bingo!'

She broke into a wide grin of her own, and excitement helped her up the rock almost as quickly as him. They stood facing the cave entrance. Cool air that had never felt the touch of the sun brushed gently against their faces.

'I don't suppose Pindari had a torch?' Brihony asked.

Beck rummaged through the pockets of the bag and his hands closed around a metal tube. 'Turns out he did.' He flicked it on. 'There's a difference between preferring the old ways and just ignoring the modern world out of stubbornness.'

They made their way forward. The floor sloped gently upwards, and the rocky walls closed in around them. Beck felt the roof brush against his hair.

After a few paces, when they were almost completely enclosed by rock, the cave turned abruptly.

They looked round the corner, and Beck shone the torch into a void. Both of them let out a whistle.

The passage opened up into a huge chamber. It was the size of a house and the shape of a giant pumpkin. The roof was held up by a natural pillar of rock. And from floor to ceiling, the curved walls were covered with paintings.

Humans and animals jostled for space on the rock face. They were all shapes and sizes, mostly smaller than life, though on the pillar facing the entrance were a couple of large figures brandishing spears as if guarding the entrance.

Figures with spears hunted herds of animals around the cave. Where the rock curved and bulged, the paintings seemed to ripple. The images were painted in shades of red and brown and looked as fresh as if they'd been done yesterday.

Beck and Brihony walked slowly into the cavern, as reverently as if it was a great temple. This place had to be unique, Beck thought. All over Australia there was rock art left by the Aboriginal peoples but he had never heard of anything like this, all in one place. Everyone would want to know about it.

Everyone deserved to. This was part of Australia's heritage.

'Beck . . .' Brihony's voice sounded strangely strangled as she studied one particular image. A group of hunters circled around an animal that Beck recognized immediately. It dwarfed them. 'This is a giant kangaroo.'

'Yeah, I can see that.'

'No, I mean, that's its name. The giant kangaroo was part of Australia's megafauna – huge animals that lived thousands of years ago. All extinct now.'

Beck remembered that Al's award had something to do with the extinction of the megafauna. He wondered what his uncle would make of this place.

'It was three metres tall,' Brihony went on. 'And there – that's a dromornis.' Beck followed her pointing finger. It looked to him like a giant dodo, but it towered over the humans attacking it. 'It was a giant flightless bird. But, Beck, the megafauna have been extinct for at least forty thousand years. So if these were painted by people who had actually seen them . . .'

Beck whistled. The paintings were unimaginably old.

'Pindari wasn't wrong,' he said. 'If the stick's here, then the ancestors really *are* watching over it.'

'So, yes – the stick. Where is it?' Brihony wondered.

'Ah. Yes . . .' Beck gazed around the interior of the cave. The paintings were awesome, but they had waited forty thousand years; they could wait a bit longer. Where was the stick? He shone the torch up and down over every inch of rock, bringing light where so little light had entered for many thousands of years. They walked right round the central pillar. Behind it, a narrow passage twisted and wound away into the depths of the earth. Beck flashed the light down there too. The paintings stopped after a few metres, and then there was nothing but bare rock. It narrowed to a crack that was too small to accommodate a person. He hoped the stick wasn't down there . . .

Beck thought for a while: maybe the instruction to follow the spears still applied in the cavern? But without even moving his head he could see ten, twenty, thirty spears all pointing in different directions.

He and Brihony returned to the entrance, where they had started. Once again Beck studied the two life-size images on the pillar that held up the roof: a man and a woman who stood facing the entrance. If you had a light, then they were the first thing you saw when you came in. Each held an upright spear, but the one on the left leaned a little to the right, while the one on the right leaned to the left. If you extended the line from the tip of each spear, the two would meet . . . Beck shone the torch at the spot where they would cross, and squinted closely up at it. There was a dark shadow in the rock there – a small recess.

'Hold this . . .' He gave the torch to Brihony so she could shine it where he was looking. Taking great care not to disturb any of the paintings with his hands or feet, he climbed a little way up the rock wall until the shadow was just above him. It was a hole about the width of a clenched fist. He couldn't see how far into the rock it went. He pushed the machete gently into the dark space, because even in a sacred place like this there might be something poisonous lurking . . .

Chapter 26

'This is the most astonishing . . .' Barega breathed. His eyes and torch darted from painting to painting. 'I mean, the most . . . the most—'

'Cut it out, Barega. Beck, I'll have the stick, thank you very much,' snapped Ganan.

Barega didn't seem to have heard him. 'How old is this place? It must be . . .'

'Forty thousand years,' Brihony said, for his benefit.

'Wow . . .'

'Beck!' Ganan barked. 'The stick!'

Beck looked from the gun, to the stick, to the gun again. 'Come and get it?' he suggested.

But Ganan stayed safely out of range. He had learned his lesson. He swung the gun round to point straight at Brihony's face. 'I'll count to five, and then Miss Stewart doesn't have a head. One, two, three—'

'OK, OK!' Beck chucked the stick so that it landed at Ganan's feet.

The man smiled and swung the gun back towards him. Beck's heart pounded as he stared down the small, dark circle of the barrel.

'And drop that machete. Now,' Ganan ordered.

Beck let it clatter to the floor.

Ganan grinned without mirth. 'You and me, kid, we've got unfinished business, and I'm going to put that right.' His finger tightened on the trigger. Beck closed his eyes, then opened them again and stared hard into Ganan's. If he was going to die, he was going to watch his death coming.

The man bit his lip. 'Turn round.'

'You can do it facing me,' Beck said through clenched teeth.

The gun wavered, and Ganan started to breathe heavily. 'I said, *turn round*!'

'To make it easier for you? I don't think so,' Beck replied. There was nowhere to run – Ganan would just shoot him in the back. He wondered if he would feel the bullet before it killed him.

Brihony let out a whimper of fear or anger or both – but then she hurled her water bottle through the air. It struck Ganan in the face, the gun went off with a roar that echoed around the cavern, and Ganan staggered back with a curse. Beck felt the bullet crack through the air past his head.

Then Brihony grabbed his hand and pulled him towards the entrance, but Barega was blocking their way. Brihony swerved and they took cover behind the pillar.

It was futile. They were running – just like the last time Ganan had tried to kill them – except that now there was nowhere to run. The men didn't even have to chase them.

That didn't stop Brihony. She ran towards the crevice they had seen earlier, but suddenly a bright light shone in their eyes. Ganan had simply come round the other side of the pillar. In the dazzling torch beam, Beck could see the glint of the gun barrel.

'We've wasted enough time,' Ganan said bitterly.

'No, wait!'

The voice came from behind them, and they jumped. Barega had appeared from the other direction; he seemed to have woken up to the fact that a murder was about to be committed.

He pushed past Beck and Brihony to confront Ganan. 'This wasn't meant to be!' he shouted. 'There wasn't meant to be any killing! That wasn't what they paid us for!'

Ganan rolled his eyes. 'For the last time, cut it out! What did you think would happen? This whole place is going to be a mine – got that? It's going to be levelled. We'll be *rich*!'

'But . . . but . . .' Barega stammered hopelessly. 'The Jungun and this place . . . and—'

'The Jungun can move out of the Stone Age or drop dead,' Ganan said harshly. 'If erasing this place helps them, then we're doing everyone a favour.' As he spoke, he lowered the gun slightly. Beck gathered himself for a leap, but Ganan reacted first, and pointed the gun straight at him.

'*No!*' shouted Barega as he leaped towards Ganan's arm just as he pulled the trigger. The gun-shot echoed around the cave and drowned out the sound of the bullet whistling into the dark. The two men grappled with each other, staggering around the cavern like a pair of drunks. Beck looked down at himself, not quite believing he was still alive. In a sudden panic, he glanced over at Brihony. Had the bullet hit her?

But she was checking herself over in the same way. 'Let's get out while they're occupied,' she said quietly.

Beck nodded, and they began to edge round the side of the cave, keeping well away from the struggling men.

And then there was another gunshot. Barega and Ganan froze, as if the music of their drunken dance had stopped. Ganan slumped forward into Barega's arms. Barega let go, and his friend toppled to the floor like a puppet whose strings had been cut. He landed with a dull thud, dark red blood staining the front of his T-shirt. Blank eyes stared up at the roof of the cave.

Barega stepped back, trembling, the gun in his hand. Then he ran to the mouth of the cave and, with a wordless, animal cry, threw it away with all his strength. After a moment Beck heard the faint splash as it hit the water.

Breathing heavily, Barega came slowly back into the cave. Beck gave Brihony a gentle nudge in one direction while he went in the other. If the man planned to attack them, then it would be harder for him if they split up.

But Barega just dropped to the ground by Ganan's body. He knelt there, his shoulders shaking with sobs.

After a while he turned his tear-stained face up to the two friends. 'I'm not going to harm you.' His voice was broken. He took the memory stick and thrust it towards Beck. 'Boat's outside. Take this, go home and show it to the world. Send the police back to arrest me when you're done.'

'Arrest you?' Beck stared down at him. 'You're not coming now?'

Barega shook his head. 'I have to make my peace with my ancestors. Just leave. Please?'

Brihony and Beck glanced at each other. Then Beck touched Barega on the shoulder, and he and Brihony headed for the entrance and looked down.

Sure enough, the boat with its patched bow was moored at the water's edge. Beck took one last look back. Barega hadn't moved. He still knelt, head bowed, next to the body of the man he had killed.

Beck turned to follow Brihony out into the light.

Epilogue

The gleaming red bus pulled up outside the Tourist Information Centre with a hiss of hydraulic brakes. Passengers were already shuffling down the aisle towards the door. Brihony and Beck waited outside in the company of the police officer who had officially looked after them since they got back to Broome. And then Beck's face broke into a grin and he waved as his uncle emerged into the sunlight.

Al waved back and came over, dragging his suitcase behind him. 'Good to see you, boy.' He wrapped his arms around Beck in a tight hug, then shook hands with the policeman. 'I'll take it from here, thanks. We'll get a taxi.'

The officer smiled and left them. The moment the policeman's back was turned, Al abruptly rapped

Beck on the back of his hand with his knuckles.

'Ow!'

'That's for being crazy enough to go off into the Outback with a couple of strangers and put yourself in danger, and . . . and . . . For crying out loud, boy, can't you see how grey my hair is? Do you want it to go *white*?'

'Yeah, well, they told me . . .' Beck's voice trailed away. He had already given Al the facts over the phone. He had *tried* to stay behind. It wasn't his fault the men had lied to him and tricked him into coming with them. Though his uncle had every right to be worried, and angry.

But Al still had one arm around his shoulder, and Beck knew that however angry his uncle had been, he was still forgiven.

'And you must be Brihony.' Al held out his hand.

'That's me. And my mum's already chewed me out, so you can save yourself the bother.'

Al smiled. 'Well, then, let's go and see her, shall we?'

'Do you know how many chemicals there are in that thing?' Beck asked.

Brihony's mouth was pursed around the straw that disappeared into her milkshake from the hospital canteen. She shook her head and sucked until the last drops had disappeared. 'And I don't care.' She smacked her lips. 'If the truck that delivered it drove past a cow, that's quite close enough to nature. No more grubs and wee for me!'

'Oh, sweetheart, please!' her mother protested.

They were in Mia's room in the hospital. She was well enough to sit up in bed and have visitors, but she still had to be monitored for a few more days.

'It's starting,' said Al, and he aimed the remote at the television.

The news channel logo flashed up to a background of music, and the newsreader went straight into the main story.

'*Representatives of the Lumos Corporation have denied any involvement in the activities of two employees—*'

'Oh, yeah, right!' Brihony exclaimed.

Beck frowned thoughtfully. He had run into powerful corporations before. They always had a way out. Only the little people got punished.

He had expected it, but it was still a shame. Someone had paid Ganan and Barega. Someone had decided that Lumos's plans were worth murdering for. It would have been good to see that someone brought to justice as well.

'*It is understood that one of the two rogue employees died when they turned on each other. The remaining man is cooperating with the police and has agreed to be tried by Circle Court—*'

'Yes!' Mia and Brihony said it together.

'What's that?' Beck asked.

'Aboriginal justice,' Al explained. 'The courts here are based on European traditions – white man's traditions. But the Circle Court is a way of bringing in the traditions of the Aboriginal people. Barega will go back to his community and be tried by a circle of representatives – tribal elders. They'll work out the most appropriate punishment. In Barega's case, I expect it will be to work for the Jungun.'

'So no jail?' Beck asked in surprise.

'Jail is a European concept. Believe me, for someone like Barega, it will be much harder to face his own people. Ganan couldn't have done it – it's not available to murderers – but we told the police that Barega tried to stop him. So he isn't officially a murderer, just a man who did wrong.'

'*Now to our other big story tonight – the discovery of what is already thought to be the largest collection of prehistoric rock art ever found in Australia. We go over to our reporter . . .*'

The reporter was on a boat in the middle of the river. Behind him some men were climbing down from the entrance of the cave. He stared excitedly at the camera and spoke into his microphone.

'*We have just heard that the Prime Minister has confirmed that the government will apply for this cave and the surrounding area to be declared a World Heritage Site. It's far too soon to say, of course, but if even a tiny bit of what we've heard about the interior of the cave is correct, then there will be no question . . .*'

Beck felt a big grin tugging at his mouth. Al caught his eye and looked equally pleased. If the cave was declared a World Heritage Site, the land would be protected for ever. Not even Lumos's billions could change that. It would be like levelling

Stonehenge to build a new shopping mall. It wasn't going to happen. The Jungun land was safe. Somewhere, somehow, Beck knew that Pindari was feeling extremely pleased. He might even allow himself a smile.

'I can't wait to see inside that cave,' Al mused. 'From what I've been hearing, it bears out all my theories.' Beck remembered the award Al had been given in Darwin: that was the whole reason for their visit. 'I've been trying to prove that the Aboriginal ancestors and the megafauna lived together for longer than scientists used to think.'

'They still drove them to extinction in the end,' Brihony pointed out.

'Yes, they did,' Al agreed solemnly. 'It's a harsh fact, but there's no sense brushing it under the carpet. It's never too late to learn from the mistakes of the past.'

On the TV, the reporter had handed back to the anchorman in the studio.

'*Now back to the main story . . .*'

Yeah, Beck thought glumly. *Back to the main story*. The main story was that there were people out there whose only aim was to exploit people and cultures and to steal money. They didn't care who they hurt to get it, or what lies they had to tell.

Beck had been thinking a lot about lies lately. He knew that a bad man makes a lie believable by mixing it with the truth. Ganan and Barega had told him a bunch of mixed-up truth and lies. The true bit had been about the pollution, and Lumos wanting to buy Jungun land. The lies had been about them wanting to fight the corporation. And in between, there had been the revelations about how Beck's parents had died. Was that lies? Was that true?

Right now, Beck was sure of only two things: that Pindari and his parents would be proud of him some-how; and that along with the ancient rock art there lived on something even more precious – knowledge of the land.

And for that, Beck felt both humbled and grateful to his mum, his dad and Pindari.

FINDING WATER

In *Claws of the Crocodile*, Beck has to carefully ration his water supplies as he travels across the Australian Outback. Finding water can be one of the greatest challenges in the wild. In the right weather you can collect rainwater, which as long as it goes into a clean vessel, will generally be safe to drink without purifying.

But what if you don't have the benefit of a water source or a full rain cloud? The good news is that water exists in even the most arid environments – you just have to know how to get your hands on it. If you think about it, it makes sense: all forms of life, including plants, need water to survive. So if you see greenery, there's water somewhere. Here are two ways of collecting it.

Above-ground solar still

Making a solar still relies on the principle of condensation. When you have a shower at home, the warm water vapour hits a cold window or mirror and turns back into liquid water. Solar stills do the same thing, only the window is a plastic bag and the shower-head is a plant.

To make a solar still, you need some green, non-poisonous vegetation. Fill a clear plastic bag about three-quarters full with the vegetation, then tie the mouth of the bag tightly. Put the bag in direct sunlight. As the plant photosynthesizes (the process of turning carbon dioxide into oxygen and water) the leaves will give off water vapour. As the water vapour hits the plastic bag, it reverts to liquid water, which you can then collect. Set up several of these stills, though, as you don't get much water from each one.

Below-ground solar still

A below-ground still also uses the principle of condensation and is a good way of extracting water from ground that you know contains moisture.

Dig a hole about a metre across and 60cm deep. Place a clean container at the bottom of the hole, making an indentation to keep it upright. If you have a length of tubing, place one end in the container and the other outside the hole so you can drink the water you collect without having to disturb the still.

Lay a piece of plastic sheeting over the hole, covering the edge with rocks, soil or sand to keep it in place. Now place a rock in the centre of the plastic. You want the plastic to be about 40cm below ground level and for the rock to be directly above the container. Moisture from the earth will condense on the bottom of the plastic sheet and drip directly into your container. Again, several stills will give you more water.

BEAR'S SECRET SCOUTING TIPS

To get more water from a below-ground solar still, line the hole with green, non-poisonous vegetation. If you do this, you might need to dig a slightly bigger hole; but as you're mixing the techniques used by both solar stills, you should get considerably more water. You can also pee into the earth around the container to make the still as damp as possible. The process of condensation will turn the moisture in your urine into clean drinking water.

BEAR GRYLLS is one of the world's most famous adventurers. After spending three years in 21 SAS he set off to explore the globe in search of even bigger challenges. He has climbed Mount Everest, crossed the Arctic in a small boat and explored deserts, jungles and swamps worldwide. His TV shows have been seen by more than 1.2 billion viewers in more than 150 countries. In 2009, Bear became Chief Scout to the Scouting Association. He lives in London on a barge and on a small island in Wales with his wife Shara and their three sons: Jesse, Marmaduke and Huckleberry.

MISSION SURVIVAL

GOLD OF THE GODS

Would you survive?

Beck Granger is lost in the jungle with no food,
no compass, and no hope of rescue.

But Beck is no ordinary teenager – he's
the world's youngest survival expert.
If anyone can make it out alive, he can.

MISSION SURVIVAL

WAY OF THE WOLF

Would you survive?

A fatal plane crash. A frozen wilderness.

The world's youngest survival expert

is in trouble again . . .

MISSION SURVIVAL

SANDS OF THE SCORPION

Would you survive?

Beck Granger is about to face his toughest survival
challenge yet – the Sahara Desert. Blistering sun
and no water for hundreds of miles . . .

Can he survive the heat and make it out alive?

TRACKS

OF THE TIGER

Would you survive?

A volcano eruption leaves Beck stranded
and alone in the jungle. Beck must use
all his skills to survive the dangers of
the jungle – can he get to safety?

MUD, SWEAT AND TEARS

This is the thrilling story of everyone's favourite
real-life action man – Bear Grylls.

Find out what it's like to take on mountaineering,
martial arts, parachuting, life in the SAS – and all
that nature can throw at you!